C000192782

ALSO BY

MASSIMO CARLOTTO

The Goodbye Kiss
Death's Dark Abyss

THE FUGITIVE

Massimo Carlotto

THE FUGITIVE

*Translated from the Italian
by Antony Shugaar*

Europa
editions

Europa Editions
116 East 16th Street
New York, N.Y. 10003
www.europaeditions.com
info@europaeditions.com

Copyright © 1994 by Edizioni e/o
First Publication 2007 by Europa Editions

Translation by Antony Shugaar
Original Title: *Il fuggiasco*
Translation copyright © 2007 by Europa Editions

All rights reserved, including the right of reproduction
in whole or in part in any form

Library of Congress Cataloging in Publication Data is available
ISBN 978-1-933372-25-9
ISBN 1-933372-25-7

Carlotto, Massimo
The Fugitive

Book design by Emanuele Ragnisco
www.mekkanografici.com

Printed in Italy
Arti Grafiche La Moderna – Rome

CONTENTS

To Silvia Baraldini

NOTE

The verses at the beginning of the first chapter are taken from the drama *Nessuno* ("No One"), by Luciano Nattino and Antonio Catalano, of the Alfieri Theater Company in Asti. The verses at the beginning of each of the other chapters are taken from songs by Stefano Maria Ricatti (from the CD *Blu*—Rossodisera Records), a Venetian singer and songwriter, and a long-time friend of mine. I am especially fond of his recordings, which kept me company through countless sleepless nights. More generally, I would like to express my appreciation to the many artists who, over the years, gave me their support, friendship, and solidarity.

I have an awkward past. It took me five large wooden crates to set my past aside and finally think of the future. In a full week of painstaking work, I filed away two hundred and twelve pounds of documents—court records, thousands of letters and telegrams, hundreds of newspaper and magazine articles, dozens of videotapes of Italian TV programs—from *Telefono giallo* and *Portobello* to *Mixer* and *Il coraggio di vivere*. Those five crates are now stored in my cellar. They are an archive of the last eighteen years of my life. Nearly half of my life.

I am a notorious legal case, the "Carlotto case." When someone happens to recognize me on the street, on a train, on a plane, they exclaim: "Hey, you're the Carlotto case!" I hold the dubious distinction of being the longest and most drawn-out case in the history of Italian justice, as well as the most controversial. Moreover, I am studied in universities as a "worst case." A unique case, never to be repeated. No Italian citizen will ever be able to wend his or her way through the same judicial labyrinth. It is now technically impossible.

And that makes me a human interest story. An extremely rare instance of systematic and relentless persecution by fate itself. Fate, in all its swindling cynicism. Though I doubt jinxes are contagious, I felt it was only fair to the reader to offer complete disclosure concerning this crucial aspect of my story, so you can make an impartial and fully informed decision whether or not to go on reading.

Everything imaginable happened to me between January 20, 1976, when I walked into a Carabinieri station to report a murder, and April 7, 1993, the day the President of the Italian Republic decided to put an end to my case with an official pardon.

I spent six years in prison, I was put through eleven different trials in the highest and lowest courts of the Italian judicial system (all the way up to Italy's supreme Constitutional Court, and at every level along the way), with the involvement of eighty-six magistrates and fifty court-appointed experts. I came very close to dying of a disease I contracted in prison.

The various courts that tried me expressed a remarkably varied array of opinions concerning my innocence or guilt, and while they were at it, those opinions lavished vitriol on the other judges. The last court to try me had the last word, and in its view I was very, but very guilty. In their written opinion, the judges stated that "with this judgment of conviction, the Court wishes to make the 'Carlotto case' a worthy episode in Italian judicial history." A bizarre assessment of my case, shared by only a few others who see my story as a shining example of judicial protection of my civil rights, given the astonishing number of verdicts. The more trials, the greater the sheer quantity of justice.

Not so. I differ with the court, of course, since I have always considered myself very, but very innocent, but I also believe there is an unbridgeable gap between reality and the way justice is administered. That argument remains relevant and is frequently and vigorously debated, while I wait for the European Court of Human Rights in Strasbourg to decide who is ultimately right.

This autobiographical account is not, in any case, about the trial; it tells the story of how the undersigned experienced for a number of years the direct consequence of that trial—life on the run—and the role that it played in the last few months of his battle with the law. I wrote this book without taking myself too seriously, much as I have always tried to do over the years. It has been my self-defense against the sleep of reason and the distractability of providence. For eighteen long years, I refrained from talking about myself, lest I add elements of confusion to the battle being waged in court. I stuck to a strategy that emphasized the judicial sphere over the human dimension, in order to preserve my case as part of the heritage of all those who believe in a "just justice" (as people used to say).

I believe this was the right choice, and ultimately a successful one. Leaving aside my personal defeat in judicial terms, my case forced the Court of Cassation, Italy's highest appeals court, and the supreme Constitutional Court, to hand down two important and enlightened verdicts that finally make trials subject to review. In more general terms, my case contributed to the larger debate about the miscarriage of justice but also about sentencing, prisons as an institution, and the health issue of diseases caused by incarceration.

Very little has been written about life on the run, and what little has been written focuses chiefly on the world of organized crime. Organized, of course, among other things, to arrange for the escape of its criminal acolytes. This book, in contrast, intends to describe the daily life, the behavior, and the routine of someone who is on the run due to a convergence of random factors. A very specific type of fugitive, who poses no danger to others; who wants only to survive and avoid capture, day after day.

What were you dreaming
when you left your home
head down
legs in the air
falling into the void
open-mouthed?

M y life on the run from the law came to an end one day in January of 1985, when Melvin Cervera Sanchez, a young, well-born lawyer with great expectations, decided to put an end to our professional relationship by selling me to the Federales.

He was my *coyote*. In Mexico, if you want to obtain any kind of official document (even documents that you have every right to request, say, for instance, because you are Mexican), it is necessary to use the services of one of these gentlemen, called *coyotes* for their widely acknowledged human decency and professional rectitude; in exchange for money, a coyote will solve whatever problems you may be having with the state bureaucracy. You should not confuse the *coyote* with the *pollero*, another figure of great national stature. The *pollero* arranges for illegal entry into the Estados Unidos. The *pollero* charges more than the *coyote;* he demands all of his clients' possessions in exchange for his services, and then packs them into broken-down trucks. Nine times out of ten, he then abandons them in the middle of the desert (on the Mexican side of the border, of course), or else near border crossings patrolled by American border agents, who have been warned in advance, because the *pollero* loves to be paid in dollars.

I decided to turn to a *coyote* because I was fed up with traveling around the world on tourist visas. I wanted to settle in one place and achieve the dream of every fugitive from the law: to be reborn, with a different identity, and start a new life.

Love had brought me to Mexico. That is, my girlfriend at the time, Alessandra, disliked all the countries I had lived in prior to Mexico. Alessandra lived in Italy and from time to time she would visit me, staying just long enough to decide that she didn't like the place and that she would never—never!—live there. Ours was a great and passionate love. It ended the day I was arrested, and I never saw her again after that. I recently learned that she married a salesman and now lives in a small village named Mattarello, in the region of Trentino. Maybe that explains why she never wanted to live in cities like Paris, Barcelona, and Lisbon.

I decided to try Mexico after reading Victor Serge's *Memoirs of a Revolutionary*. Serge had been a militant anarchist in France before living through the October Revolution as a Bolshevik. He was subsequently swept up in Stalin's purges and, after a lengthy stay in Siberia, he finally made his way to the land of the unfinished revolution.

Alessandra really loved the book. I wasn't as enthusiastic, but I was still fascinated by the description of this country, a place filled with sunshine, tequila, tortillas, and *revolución*. I will confess that winding up in Mexico City, with its population of twenty-one million, its pollution, constantly threatening immediate evacuation of the city, and the total careening lunacy of an out-of-control megalopolis—it is in fact roundly considered to be one of the most unlivable cities on earth—slightly dampened my initial enthusiasm.

Melvin Cervera Sanchez seemed like the right person for the job. He was the brother-in-law of a prominent left-wing intellectual who had taken my case to heart. He had all the social and professional attributes to help me become a Mexican. My intellectual friend introduced us at a party. The following day, in his law office, Melvin outlined his plan of action to me and presented me with a bill for his services. A staggering sum. I assumed that paying in advance was just a quaint local custom.

I also considered for a moment the possibility that he might be planning to screw me, but I immediately ruled it out because, in Italy, if someone is caught helping you in any way, shape, or form to acquire Italian citizenship illegally, the consequences can be quite serious. Relatives included. Anyway, I assumed he would never cause me problems because of my friendship with his brother-in-law. That was my clinching argument for relying on Melvin. But things in Mexico seem to work differently.

Melvin's plan was brilliant. He was going to bring back to life the son—who had died an untimely death—of an Italian emigrant couple. The certificate of civil status of this latter-day Lazarus would make its way from one bureaucratic agency to another, progressively acquiring the trappings of an honorable discharge from military service and other such documents, until the reborn son was finally registered to vote. I was so excited about the various details of the plan that when Melvin insisted on accompanying me back to my apartment, I wasn't suspicious in the least. That night, I dropped off to sleep for the first time without any worries about what the next day would bring. But my awakening couldn't have been ruder. Strange men with gassed-back hair and dark sunglasses swarmed into my bedroom, armed and short-tempered.

What astonished me, more than the simple fact of the betrayal, was their belief that I was a terrorist and a member of the Red Brigades. To inflate the price for turning me over, that well-known kidder, Melvin Cervera Sanchez, had warned the Federales that I was a dangerous fugitive and Red Brigades militant. When it dawned on me what a horrible turn matters could take, I was so frightened that I told the police my real name. In a nightmarish twist of fate, my name was practically the same as that of an Italian Red Brigades terrorist who was wanted in Mexico for the murder of two policemen.

Things went from bad to worse. They took me to Calle de Soto, the notorious headquarters of the Mexican political police. They held me there for ten days, and beat me black and blue. I have never been very good at dealing with the police. I always come off as a smart-ass, and whenever I claim to be innocent, not only am I generally not believed, but it tends to make my questioner lose his patience. I also have a special gift for creating misunderstandings in the dialogue. This tends to stoke the already simmering anger of the police, whose sole aim is to pry loose a nice solid confession and go home, happy to have earned their salary.

The first thing that made me unpopular with the Federales was my surname.

"What is your name, *cabrón*?"

"Massimo Carlotto."

"Your whole name, *hijo de puta*!"

"Massimo Carlotto, like I just told you."

"Is Carlotto your father's surname or your mother's?"

"My father's."

"What's your mother's surname?"

"Villani."

"In that case, *cabrón y hijo de puta*, your name is Massimo Carlotto Villani."

"No, Señor Detective, my name is Massimo Carlotto, and if my name was Massimo Carlotto Villani, I would be somebody else."

"What do you mean somebody else?"

"That's right. Massimo Carlotto is my name. If you say Massimo Carlotto Villani, it's not me anymore."

"Take him away! This *pendejo* wants to be a wise-ass. He needs a little more of our special treatment," the detective roared, turning purple in the face.

While his subordinates worked diligently and with consummate skill to give my face a new appearance, it dawned on me where the misunderstanding had arisen: in Mexico, in contrast with the way things are done in Italy, everyone has a double surname. I tried to interrupt the special treatment to explain, but it was too late. Say what you want about the Mexican police, but you can't deny that they obey orders to the letter. When I was finally able to speak to the detective, though I was slurring my words by then, I managed to clear up the misunderstanding.

The second question was about my age. There too an unfortunate misunderstanding arose, and the policemen had to start their work all over again. In ten days' time, the police only managed to set down two pages of legal transcripts. In brief, it was an unpleasant experience. I only think back on it when I piss and I notice the whitish scars that the electrodes left on my dick.

And so, for a long time, I hated Melvin and his entire family. No longer. Time, we all know, is a gentleman and heals all wounds. Bygones are bygones and, more to the point, Melvin is dead.

I learned of the "tragic" event in 1987, during my extended stay in the Padua house of detention. One day, I received a letter from Mexico with a newspaper clipping. It reported the news of the murder of the young lawyer, "hit by *cinco balazos* from a .45 caliber pistol, as he was leaving his house." The article ventured the hypothesis that the murder was a revenge killing by the Salvadoran guerrillas of the Frente Farabundo Martí, annoyed at Melvin's customary entrepreneurial approach to business. Apparently, in fact, in one of his last professional endeavors, Melvin had arranged to sell out a group of political refugees to the El Salvador secret police.

I still don't understand, to this day, what mysterious mechanism transformed me, on my tenth day in Calle de Soto, from a dangerous terrorist into an undesirable alien, to be expelled from the country as quickly as possible. In a single busy morning, the police managed to hustle me over to a doctor's office, where I was stitched back together, to the Migración office, to procure the necessary documents for my expulsion, to a laundry where my clothes were cleaned (all the clothing that I had at home, as well as my other personal effects, was already the property of the Federales), to a hotel, where I took a shower, and finally to the KLM office, to buy a plane ticket back to Italy.

I could have traveled anywhere in the world I wanted; I could have started all over again from scratch. But my experience in Mexico had taken its toll, and to wage a battle in court, even if I was doing it from a jail cell, didn't seem like such a bad prospect. At least, not at the time.

That same afternoon, I was flying back to Milan's Linate Airport, via Amsterdam. During the boarding process, my status as an *expulsado* was brought to the attention of passengers and crew. While the Federales were eager to slip yours truly into an economy seat as quickly as possible and be rid of me, the airport police insisted that I pay the required expatriation tax. When I informed the airport police that my police escort had already robbed me of everything I owned, including my money, they took the position that the Federales had to pay the exit tax. Words began to fly and tensions were rising. The argument was finally settled by a steward who took me by the arm and hustled me down the aisle to the seat that had been reserved for me.

I was sitting next to an English girl traveling with her parents; they were returning to Liverpool after a long vacation in the Yucatan. She spoke good Spanish; the scene with the Federales had aroused her curiosity, and she started asking me about what had happened. I gave her a revised and corrected version of events. I couldn't bring myself to tell her that I was flying back to a jail cell, with fifteen years of "time-to-serve" ahead of me.

She seemed to like me, and she was in the mood to talk. I stared at her hungrily; I knew that for years and years to come,

I would think back on this rare opportunity to be close to a woman. I savored every move she made, every word she said. After the stopover in Chicago, she fell asleep and I continued to stare at her. But there was no room in my mind for her now. My mind was teeming with all the memories of prison that I had tried to wipe away over the years.

I was a prisoner once again. Gradually, as the hours ticked by, prison became increasingly real. I could even smell it; the unmistakable sounds filled my ears. Slamming gates, shouting, keys turning in locks. And the silence, so unnatural and freighted with despair that I would startle awake in those first few months. When I was nineteen. Then, I turned twenty. Twenty-one. Then freedom. Acquitted and convicted. Convicted again. Escaped. And now, at twenty-nine, I was flying back to it all.

I had to change planes in Amsterdam; while waiting for my flight I phoned my family. My mother answered the phone. A woman of honey and steel. Hearing her voice left me breathless and for a moment, I couldn't help thinking that, at least, I was going home.

"Ciao, Mamma, it's Massimo."

"Ciao Massimo, we're coming to Milan."

"You know all about it?"

"Yes, they told us."

"Mamma, what now?"

"We're going to fight for a new trial." Prophetic words.

There's no end to bad news. When I arrived in Milan, without papers, and with an expulsion decree in hand, I held out my wrists to the border police, thus informing them of my intention to turn myself in. It was a stunning blow to learn that there was no warrant for my arrest, much less an international all-points bulletin. I had lived for years like a hunted animal, while no one at all was looking for me, not even back home. That's injustice for you. They took me to San Vittore prison all the same and there, thirteen days later, I was handed a warrant. At last. I was starting to wonder if I had just dreamed all those trials.

What had happened was that they had drawn up a warrant for my arrest, but then it had lain forgotten in a drawer somewhere. If I hadn't come back to Italy it would probably have stayed there forever, considering that it took them thirteen days to find it.

So while this marked the end of my life as a fugitive from justice, it also marked the beginning of my years as a prison inmate. It wasn't easy to get used to the change. Every so often I would behave as if I was still on the run. Once I tried to pass myself off as the convict from the cell next door, who was due for release. I cut that out pretty quickly though; the prison guards made it clear that it was a bad idea.

During my long battle in the courts, which was to continue for another eight years until April 7, 1993, people often asked me to talk about that particular part of my life, when I found myself living as an accidental fugitive. I told most of the people who asked that it had been a horrible experience that I wouldn't wish upon my worst enemies. If someone insisted on trying to dig deeper and asked me to define the concept of life on the run, I would answer that "life on the run is like the blues: it's a state of mind."

I can't claim credit for this definition, but I adopted it to respect an ethical commitment that I had made to the one, brief friendship that I made in Calle de Soto. I had a German cell mate there. I never learned his name, or why he had left Germany and come to Mexico. All I know is, as a fugitive, he left a lot to be desired. Trying to travel around Central America with the physique of a Viking, light-blue eyes, platinum blond hair, a totally unworkable accent, and a Guatemalan passport made out to a certain Ramón is truly the mark of a reckless fool. He had been there since the evening of the day before. When the Federales opened the cell door to put me in, there he stood, before me. That was the one time I got a good look at him because the cell was dark and, for only a couple hours a day, depending on the position of the sun, a faint shaft of light shone through the slits in the door, illuminating strips of wall. As soon as he opened his mouth and began peppering me with questions, I realized that he wasn't much of a jailbird, either.

"Listen carefully, my friend," I said to him. "I don't know who you are, and I don't want to know. And I really don't want to answer your questions. The only topic of conversation in here will be life inside this cell. By the way, have you looked around to see what there is in here?"

"There's nothing in here," he replied, "just a broken toilet."

"You need to know how to look," I said, and started feeling around with both hands, exploring the cracks in the floor, walls, and toilet. Ten minutes later, I had found a cigarette, three matches, and a pencil stub, and I had killed all the insects I could lay my hands on.

"Somebody broke the toilet so that you can get drinking water when you push the flush-button. It must mean that they won't give us much water in here," I informed my German cell mate. Then I asked him: "Did you find any graffiti on the wall?"

"No, why?"

"The hidden cigarette butt. Whoever was in here before us left it so that those who came after could leave a message. Then, whoever gets a chance passes the messages on. You ever been in jail before?"

"No."

"It shows."

I dug around in my pocket and found a Kleenex, carefully

rolled it up, and sacrificed one of my three precious matches to turn it into a jury-rigged torch. I was thus able to read some of the graffiti on the wall. It was just as I had said: they were all identical—first name, last name, date of arrest, the address of a relative to be contacted. In some cases, the name of an informer or the policeman who made the arrest.

"Shall we smoke the cigarette?" he asked me.

"Do you already know how often the guards go by?"

"No."

"Then we'll wait and figure it out. If they see us smoking or smell it, they'll beat the shit out of us."

The cell was suffocatingly hot, and we moved as little as possible, dressed only in our underwear. He talked the whole time. I ignored him as much as I was able. His endless jabbering about life, people, and nature kept me from thinking. My brain was already feverish with the effort to come up with a reason to keep the grease-heads from crushing my balls again.

The phrase about the blues being a state of mind came out like this: "Ramón" suddenly grabbed one of my arms and, staring me straight in the eyes, said: *"Mano"* (Mexican slang for *hermano*, or 'brother') and then all the rest. I thought to myself that he had lost it from the heat, and I hissed at him, threateningly: *"Callate!"* (Shut up.)

I regretted it the next day. He was in pretty bad shape when they brought him back from questioning; he died during the night, while I was asleep, but he was still with me for three more days, until I managed to bribe a guard with the gold chain that my mother had given me. When the light of the sun filtered back through the cracks in the door and illuminated the wall, I extracted my pencil stub from its hidey-hole and wrote the epitaph of:

"Ramón"—male, German, died during the days following 21 January 1985, alert the German embassy.

I decided that that was a good time to smoke the cigarette

butt, and I savored it without haste, waiting for dark to fall again. I considered writing something about myself, but all I could think of were high-flown phrases, ill-suited for a cell in Calle de Soto, so I decided to skip the idea entirely.

Nowadays, my sense of guilt makes me think that the German's flow of words had been nothing more or less than a sort of spiritual last will and testament, which I had refused to hear.

I've only gotten really drunk a very few times in my life. Once when I read in the newspaper that, following the massive earthquake that hit Mexico City, a rescue team of excavators had found in the basement of Calle de Soto the corpses of a number of people who had been tied up and tortured. The government of the Distrito Federal, in a transport of indignation (indignant at how thoroughly the rescue teams had done their work, more than anything else), ordered the building shut down, and some grease-head paid for the sins of all the others.

Even now, I try to stay true to my ethical commitment, and I continue to say that life on the run is a state of mind, even though I actually believe that my experience as a fugitive might be more accurately described as a sort of meta-theater of survival. As in the *commedia dell'arte*, I was a face that gave origin to a series of different masks, caricatures of clearly defined social stereotypes, improvising day by day within the context of a general plot structure which was nothing more than the intertwining details of my wending progress through the halls of justice and my own decision to become a fugitive from the law. Characters that I selected and chose: a decision to shake off the role, straight out of the legal soap opera, into which I had been typecast by the trial, both before and after I went on the run, the only role that I never figured out how to play. A role that I always rebelled against completely.

The imaginary world of those who hold, for a lifetime or a single day, absolute mastery over the life of a man demanded a character-qua-defendant midway between Totò and Alberto

Sordi: obsequious, quick to tears and panic, infinitely ridiculous, and infinitely dramatic.

I was almost always impassive, cool, and remote. In that way, I was my own worst enemy, as my lawyers often told me. Remote and impassive both with respect to the tragedy and the paradoxical comedy into which the liturgy of the court often slipped. *Épater le bourgeois* was the only possible form of rebellion when you have been cast against your will in an inexorably imposed piece of ensemble theater.

David Mamet believes that the purpose of theater is the production of meaning. My character, strident and unreal on that stage, was meant only to force its audience to be rational, to abandon political and social prejudices and engage in an objective evaluation of the facts. I asked nothing more than to be judged justly. My act didn't always play well with my audience, and the reviews (which came in the form of verdicts) often panned my performance. In the end, however, the theater company of justice decided that, cost what it may, that role would belong to me for all time, even after the production had finished its run, and no more performances were scheduled. Playing "out of character" had therefore been my way of choosing freedom.

There are various categories of fugitives. There are mobsters, politicians, businessmen, bankers, and many others, who usually have resources and enjoy levels of protection sufficient to live on the run as if it were a minor inconvenience. Of course, I belonged to none of these categories. I was a classic accidental fugitive, someone who never expected to have problems with the law, who never thought that he would need to "invent" an escape from his own country as the one way to save his own life, his freedom, and his personal dignity. The defining characteristic of the accidental fugitive is a lack of resources and protection. An accidental fugitive has absolutely no idea of how to live on the run.

When I learned that my appeal to the Court of Cassation (Italy's highest court of appeal) had been denied, and that I had to decide whether to escape or serve another fifteen years in prison, the first thing I did was burst into tears. Uncontrollable tears. Then, in a catatonic trance, I went to the train station, bought a ticket to Paris, and left the country. I crossed the border with my identity card, which no one—despite my legal situation—had thought to confiscate. I remember absolutely nothing about that trip. The decision to escape had been made so impulsively that I didn't even realize what I was doing. I couldn't string two thoughts together, because I was devastated by the news of my guilty verdict, which I had always considered an impossibility.

When my train arrived in the Gare de Lyon, I burst into tears again as soon as I set foot on the platform. I only stopped crying when a Parisian *flic* asked me if I was okay.

I stumbled into the Metro, and had a hard time getting out of the underground labyrinth. I had never seen a subway before. In Padua, we don't even take the bus very often. Everyone rides a bicycle.

Paris was the only place I could go. It has long been a destination for political exiles, and generation after generation of refugees have created a full-fledged culture of solidarity for those forced to flee their homeland. A community that has given France a great deal, in terms of intellectual and artistic growth, helping Paris to become the cosmopolitan city that it is today.

I needed help and I received it, in abundance; help that I never got the chance to pay back. I met and became friends with wonderful people, who helped me to grow as a person. I had arrived screaming my desperation as the victim of a miscarriage of justice, but when I understood the horrors that had been inflicted upon the community of Greek, Turkish, Kurdish, Argentine, Chilean, and Iranian refugees, I shut my mouth and learned the value of dignity.

To all those who helped me, I was one more problem added to the mountain of burdens they were already bearing, but no one shrank from the task. I was wanted for what was considered a common crime (though my political activity in Lotta Continua had a significant bearing on my trial) and while I was risking fifteen more years in an Italian prison, what they were facing was certainly far worse—they might well be expelled from France, one of the few nations on earth willing to offer political asylum. That was why I finally left Paris, but the network of people in which I moved remained the same.

The first and only time that I left that network, I met Melvin Cervera Sanchez.

Those who return home in the middle of the sea
those who choose not to breathe
those who cultivate an expanse of sand
those who hide behind an unmasked face

For a fugitive, the look is fundamental. It's not something you can just choose at random. It has to match the fugitive's physical appearance and need to escape with the social and cultural characteristics of the place he's chosen to hide in. For instance, showing up at the Swiss border dressed as a gypsy, a punk, a goth, or a latter-day hippie is a bad idea.

In general, the look needs to be sobersided but, first and foremost, it must respect the golden rule of life on the run, which demands that it be as reassuring as possible. It has to convey the impression to the policemen who are watching you or who have stopped you that they are just wasting their time, because it is inconceivable that anyone who looks like that could be a good-for-nothing. As a result, I was obliged to impersonate stereotypical figures from social groups quite different from the one I belonged to and frequented (and whose look left a lot to de desired).

The characters I projected served only as camouflage; they would never have withstood a more careful inspection. So I needed to do a good job of acting and lavish an obsessive care on the details. Until I went back to Italy and discovered that no one had ever dreamed of looking for me, I had always considered myself a master of disguise; then I began to have my doubts.

I copied Bernard, my first disguise, from Louis de Funès movies. He had short hair which left his ears uncovered (in the photographs in my identity documents, you can always see the ears), a goatee-style beard, neatly trimmed, fake eyeglasses with a lightweight, pseudo-tortoise-shell frame. Light-brown suits purchased at the BHV in the Rue de Rivoli, ties that were intentionally abominable, and, at any hour of the day or night, a copy of *France Soir* protruding from his overcoat or jacket pocket, depending on the season. And finally, a leather bag, of abysmal quality, carefully worn and tattered in the right places.

Even a quick glance at Bernard conveyed the impression: a) that he had a low-paid, white-collar job; perhaps he was a civil servant (especially effective were the shoes: carefully re-soled, with a crescent-shaped metal heel tap); b) that he was married with children (gold wedding band on the left ring finger, small, unobtrusive gift-wrapped packages on national holidays, and boxes of pastries on Sundays); c) that he was a picture of existential resignation and that he was politically and socially harmless; d) and that he had an inborn respect for authority and an unshakable love of his country (as demonstrated by a French tricolor badge in the buttonhole of his lapel).

I remember how I glowed with contentment when Alessandra flew to see me in Paris and, after taking a quick look at me, said, "Darling, what have you done to yourself? You look like a cop!" Unfortunately for Bernard's sex life, I still reminded her of a cop with my clothes off.

In any case, I saw proof on a daily basis that my "mask" was working perfectly. Whenever I boarded a bus or stepped onto the Metro (after a few months I had figured out how to use it), I was immediately drawn by my supposed social counterparts into a web of silent expressions of shared disapproval—signaled by complicit glances and tiny, imperceptible head-shakes—for the homeless, gypsies, or street artists whose mere existence constituted an annoyance to the respectable citizens of the city.

And if the people that I was trying to mimic identified me at a glance, so did my social antagonists. I had a chance to verify this one evening, when I took the Metro home after going out to see a movie. I happened to sit in a car that was empty except for me and a gang of *banlieusards*. They started to make fun of me and insult me as soon as I sat down and, when the train reached the Châtelet station, they beat me up and stole my wristwatch.

Next came Gustave. I planned him as the intellectual variation on Bernard, but somehow people always took him for a Belgian. I never did understand why, but maybe that's because I've never been in Belgium. Whatever the explanation, as soon as people heard me speak, they would exclaim, "Oh, so you're *not* Belgian!" I wore a large dark-blue beret, pulled down low over my forehead and then tugged back, a scarf whose color went nicely with my light-brown duffel coat and my pea-green corduroy suit with a light-wool vest, topped off with colorful bowties. Gustave was inspired by movies about the French Resistance; he was the perfect young professor of art history or music teacher, a bit of a daydreamer, who had been dressing in this same style since he was twelve (the only concession to adulthood was long pants instead of shorts). Someone without a lot of weird ideas in his head. A harmless, reassuring individual.

I came up with Gustave as a way to go out to art galleries, independent movie houses, and cafés at night without constantly being taken for a cop. This happened all the time with Bernard, and it was embarrassing to my friends. It got so bad that one evening, at La Coupole in Montparnasse, where I used to hang out on Saturday evenings to savor the Parisian milieu that Manuel Scorza (my favorite writer at the time) used to frequent, a prostitute approached me, assuring me that there was a guaranteed discount for members of the police force.

The problem with these two characters was that they weren't particularly appealing to the female sex (professionals aside). In fact, most women reacted with a certain distaste at first sight. I never ventured past this first reaction, but I have always wondered where the Bernards and the Gustaves of this world find their girlfriends, since as a rule they get married. For Gustave, I suppose that the answer is Belgium; for Bernard the question remains shrouded in mystery.

In my experience as a fugitive, I was obliged more than once to invent characters for just a few days, either because they were specially suited to a specific situation, or else because my cover of the moment had been blown.

For instance, in the summer, when I took the train across the border between France and Spain (then considered a tough border crossing because of the chronic excesses of the Basque independence movement), I would assume a disguise of such completely reassuring innocence and naïveté (even if slightly shabby) that the French and Spanish police wouldn't even ask to see my identity papers. I shaved off my goatee, cut my hair even shorter, and became Lucien the tourist. I would cross the border wearing a white tennis cap, a white "I Love New York" T-shirt, dark-blue knee-length bermuda shorts, canary yellow terry cloth socks, and a pair of white Adidas. Hanging around my neck was a leather water bag, inscribed with *Recuerdo de España* if I was coming from the Basque Country, or a canteen with the Madonna of Lourdes if I was traveling in the opposite direction. Instead of the classic backpack—a known irritant to policemen, likely to arouse suspicion and dislike—I carried a lizard-green vinyl suitcase covered with decals from youth hostels and Catholic sports associations.

My acting style consisted of a relentless cheerfulness and a total self-abnegation toward others. You know the type: he'll stand in the aisle throughout a train trip even if he got to the station an hour before departure time, because he gives his seat away to anyone who looks into the compartment; the whole time he is also helping women and old men to board and leave the car, all the while scattering phrases like "Have a good trip and enjoy your day!"

Other borders I crossed by bicycle. Mountain bikes weren't available then, and I rode a racing bike, covered with headlights, reflector disks, and luggage racks. I would arrive at the border crossing exhausted, drenched in sweat and gamy as could be (I wonder why all the border crossings I've ever seen are perched on inaccessible mountain tops), arousing in the border police that special feeling of pity that one feels toward those who like to suffer through their holidays. Often, they would make a big show of ignoring me.

The way I liked to cross borders best was illegally, over the mountains. Hiking through the woods, with a backpack on my back, filled me with a sense of happiness. It made me feel like one of the smugglers in the movie *L'amante dell'Orsa Maggiore* (*The Smugglers*).

I was forced to eliminate both Bernard and Gustave because of a phone call made over a line that might have been tapped by the police. That's right. When you are on the run, a simple "might have been" is enough to make you drop everything and start over from scratch.

The screw-up was the work of Horacio, a politically effervescent Argentine exile. I had told him a thousand times to use pay phones to call me, but he couldn't grasp the difference between an accidental fugitive and a political exile. He called to invite me to a party; I couldn't hear any noise in the background, which filled me with misgivings. "Horacio, you're calling from your house, aren't you?" I asked. The guilty silence on the other end of the line was all I needed to be certain. Fifteen minutes later I was already on my way. I pulled a folded sheet of paper out of my wallet with an emergency phone number. I stepped into the first phone booth I found and picked up the receiver.

My ace in the hole was a Greek Communist who had fled

the country when the Colonels took over. He stayed in France and enjoyed a highly successful career as a psychiatrist. I had never met him, but he knew about my situation; I told him what had happened and we made an appointment to meet near Place de la Bastille. He showed up late in a beat-up mustard-yellow Lada: a skinny little guy, about forty-five, well dressed, with a dark complexion that made him look more like a North African than a Greek. Courteous and friendly, he told me that I could use his apartment; he would sleep at his girlfriend's place until I could find another place to stay.

He just forgot to tell me that his house was located on the grounds of the psychiatric hospital where he worked, which I only found out when we drove through the main gate. It was an insane asylum for the wealthy, just outside of Paris; a handsome mansion with extensive grounds, and old stables that had been turned into a hospital. It was a private hospital that favored alternative psychiatry. The psychiatrists lived in elegant little row houses that blended into the greenery. There were tennis courts and playgrounds for children. After showing me around his home and recommending that I read a number of party documents (which I later found to be in Greek), we agreed on a plausible cover in case of indiscreet questions. We created the character of Alberto, an Italian colleague, who had come to visit him for a few days. I had never pretended to be a psychiatrist before, but the real psychiatrist told me not to worry. It's a lot harder to pretend to be a heart surgeon, he told me. It was early on a Friday afternoon, and he took his leave, saying that he'd be back on Monday, since he had no appointments till then.

About an hour later, I went over to the guard station. I wanted to go back into town to get matters back on track, though my first errand would be to give Horacio a thorough dressing down. I tapped on the glass and waited patiently while the guard finished reading an article in his sports magazine. When he finally looked up, I told him that I wanted to go out for a while. I was a friend of the Greek psychiatrist, I added, by way of explanation. The guard smiled pleasantly at me, but made no motion to buzz the gate open. I tapped on the glass a little harder, and made the same request, providing a greater array of details this time. His smile was just as benevolent as the first time, but I could tell that he had no intention of letting me out. I lost my temper. And it wasn't so much because he wouldn't open the gate to let me out; it was that the idiot refused to acknowledge that I was "sane." Pounding furiously on the glass, I found myself shouting things like "I'm a psychiatrist myself" and the classic phrase, "You have no idea who you're dealing with." At that point, he lost his temper too, as only the French know how to lose their tempers. He unleashed a torrent of foul insults and rude gestures and threatened to call the male nurses.

That's when I began to smile pleasantly at him; I waved goodbye and left. Not quite running, but moving fast, I made it back to the house. I was terrified (I could already envision myself in a straitjacket, trying to explain to muscle-bound syringe-wielding nurses that I was Alberto, a colleague of the Greek psychiatrist) and furious (enough crap had already happened to me for one day); so I headed straight for the phone, only to remember, just as I was about to dial his girlfriend's phone number, that he hadn't left it. I started to search through the house for clues of any sort that might help me to discover her identity. Nothing.

On the other hand, I found something that gave me food for thought: a shopping bag full of condoms. Greek condoms. I'd never seen anything like it. There were hundreds of condoms, enough to stock a nuclear fallout shelter. In one drawer, I found an address book that gave me a moment's hope, but evidently the guy was friends with half the population of Paris. The address book was crammed with names and phone numbers.

Before giving in to despair and accepting the idea that I was going to spend the next three days as a prisoner in an insane asylum, I decided to try my luck with a few phone calls. I singled out a series of phone numbers that corresponded to women's names without surnames, imagining that they all might be friends. The first phone call was also the last one. Monique was very adamant that the psychiatrist wasn't at her house. She only saw him once a week, since she was his patient.

Twenty-four hours later, I ran out of cigarettes. It was a terrible weekend. About ten days later, I moved out of that damned hospital and into a new place in the Place de la République neighborhood.

I had found a place to live and a job in the same area. I was working as an usher in a movie house owned by a Portuguese guy. The movie house didn't attract many customers. The movies were definitely high quality stuff, but really boring. He would schedule things like a week of Angolan film, or Vietnamese movies in the original language, with Russian subtitles. In France, the only money that ushers make comes from tips, so from time to time, I attempted to persuade the owner to show something a little more commercial, but there was so little interest in third-world cinema in Europe that the Portuguese owner, rightly, preferred political commitment to profit.

Next to the movie house was a major punk club, the Gibus. Brawls were a nightly occurrence: inside, among the clubgoers, and outside, between punks and North Africans. The neighborhood, once inhabited by middle-class families, had slowly declined through the strange urban alchemistic process typical of big cities, and even though it was in the heart of Paris, it had become cheap enough for the lowest classes of immigrants to live there. I could have afforded better, but I hadn't found anything. I was living in an apartment building that had known better days; now, however, it was a warren of studio apartments, one-room cells no bigger than two hundred square feet, swarming with rats and cockroaches, where entire families paid rents of a thousand francs a month to live in crowded squalor. I was the white tenant in the building. Gaining acceptance from my neighbors wasn't easy, nor was finding a character who would fit in with the location. A Bernard wouldn't live in a neighborhood like that one. I selected a "mask" that would work only there, and that forced me to stay in the neighborhood for months: José, a Spaniard, who wore *camperos* boots and blue jeans, a leather jacket and a dark-blue sailor's cap. He worked at the movie house, but he gave the impression that he was involved in something shady. That was to keep the neighborhood kids from robbing me every night.

I was coming home from work one night when I heard some young guys who lived in the building talking in the courtyard about teaching the punks a lesson. I was in favor of it myself; I couldn't stand the punks. I walked over and told them not to do it outside of the Gibus Club; those of us who worked at the movie house would necessarily be dragged into it, and we didn't want the police snooping around, asking questions, or even worse, a permanent police guard outside of the club. We got to talking, and a little while later I was lending them the benefit of my experience of fighting the local fascists back in the streets of Padua, laying out scenarios for potential campaigns of urban guerrilla warfare. The boys liked my ideas, and in the end we came up with a plan. In order to get the punks away from the Gibus, a small group of the fastest kids would provoke them, and then cut and run. They would draw the punks out to an isolated square, ideal for our purposes. The conditions that I had imposed—no weapons, and especially no punk "hamburgers"—were finally agreed to, however reluctantly.

The following evening, when I got home from work, I found the courtyard filled with kids, many of them accompanied by older brothers. We shook hands all around, and then moved out to our various positions. What I was doing violated all the rules of clandestine security, but I was going to have to live in that neighborhood for who knows how much longer and I wanted to be accepted. Everything went according to plan, and the enemy went down in painful defeat. As long as I lived in that neighborhood, there were no more attacks against North Africans.

When I became Jason, an English computer expert, I returned to a calmer and far more comfortable lifestyle. The cover verged on perfection; the one tiny defect was my complete ignorance of the English language and computers.

There was a real Jason, who had rented the house, through an agency, from England. One of his secretaries, who was also perfectly English, had gone to pick up the keys. No one had ever seen him (fortunately! He was short, painfully skinny, and a redhead. I could never have pretended to be him), so when I moved into the apartment, everyone immediately assumed I was him.

In order to get through my first meeting with the concierge—concierges tend to be nosy, gossipy, and duplicitous—I showed up in the company of my supposed secretary, who served as interpreter during our initial introduction. In order to limit my contacts with the concierge to hellos and goodbyes, we had decided that Jason, newly arrived from the far side of the English Channel, did not know a word of French. For the entire time that I lived in that apartment building, I said *bonjour* and *bon soir* in an accent that I had adopted from the French renditions of Laurel and Hardy. The concierge must have been about forty. When I noticed the wedding band on her finger, I wondered what her husband did for a living. He was a cop, naturally, as I deduced from his uniform. Luckily, he was a laid-back cop. Once he got home, he forgot about his work and minded his own business. The tenants were his wife's concern.

The time came to leave Paris and Europe. To get across the borders that awaited me, I went back to the guise of an Italian tourist. I didn't need a place of my own anymore, so I moved to Pigalle, where I stayed with a friend, a woman from Peru. Though the neighborhood was quite seamy, it was a perfect backdrop for the tourist disguise; there was a never-ending supply of tourists, at all hours of the day and night. There was one pitfall, however. I had to avoid bumping into tourists from Padua; before my stay in Pigalle, I had no idea of the uncontrolled passion that my fellow Paduans seemed to have for Pigalle and its sinful nightclubs, all sex and sequins. The Paduans arrived by the busload. I even ran into a high school science teacher of mine, a notorious ballbreaking prude—but now he was tipsy and giddy. Our paths crossed as I was stepping out of a smoke shop; the only reason he failed to recognize me is that he was too busy nudging his friends, excitedly calling their attention to a little cluster of whores.

The presence of Paduans around the world got me to thinking to the point of formulating the theory that wherever you go you'll find one. One who knows you well enough to recognize you. In the most godforsaken places on earth, places where a fugitive had every right to be able to relax, I was constantly falling into frenzies of panic because I had just spotted someone who could get me into trouble. Maybe not right then and there, but back home, watching the movies, my fellow Paduan might exclaim, "Hey, I know that guy!" And Paduans always seem to own the most up-to-date video equipment; after a while, I became an expert at jabbing a finger up my nose, because, as we all know, nobody wants the embarrassment of showing their friends movies of some guy picking his nose.

In Mexico I became Max, the tourist/student. It wasn't much as covers go, but there I couldn't find any other characters to play. First of all, because my physical presence and facial features were too distinct, and also because it seemed too risky to try to play a role I doubted I could impersonate very well.

Acting is a fundamental skill for a fugitive, as much as for any stage actor. When an actor is unable to inhabit his role, when he fails to bring a relaxed and natural presence to the stage, he triggers a sense of cringe-provoking embarrassment in his audience. This is true of a fugitive as well. He must inhabit his character in a relaxed and natural way; otherwise anyone who spends time with him will begin to suspect that something isn't right.

Max gave the impression that he was European, more northern than southern; because of his size and his light blue eyes, he was taken for German, Dutch, Norwegian, or French, but never for Italian. He wore casually elegant designer clothing, to distinguish him from the hippies who were generally disliked in Mexico, and in order to give the idea that he had the financial resources to deal with any unexpected development. I had to have clothing shipped to me from Europe, because I couldn't find clothes that fit me. There were no "big and large" stores at all. If Melvin hadn't betrayed me, if I had succeeded in becoming a Mexican citizen, I would have been obliged to go on a drastic diet in order to wear the costume that went with my new character. He was a university student and, at the same time, a tourist, because I was old enough to be a graduate; it was therefore fundamental to make Max look like somebody with plenty of money, someone who could afford to enjoy life in an exotic locale. In Europe, this persona wouldn't have lasted ten days, but in Central America, if you were careful, it could last for twenty years, because people are used to gringo eccentricities. The stereotype of the tourist, however, requires that the look you adopt should convey a certain prosperity, otherwise people tend to be far less tolerant.

I have frequently found myself in potentially dangerous situations, say, when the police were doing a routine ID check, and been waved through without a glance because the authorities chose to focus on those foreigners who looked like they had made the unforgivable gaffe of not bringing large amounts of prized European currency.

One time I was heading for Mexico City, traveling by bus through the Oaxaca region. Most of the passengers were locals, except for yours truly and twelve North Americans. The North Americans were barefoot, dressed in white monk's habits cinched tight at the waist with gold cords; they had long hair, and each wore a plastic crown of thorns. I was intrigued, so I asked them why they were dressed that way; they explained that they were the sect of the twelve apostles. They had left Belize and were traveling to the Mexican capital to announce some revelation or other.

The bus was pulled over at a checkpoint; an army lieutenant who boarded the bus to check the passengers' documents took one look at them and his face turned bright red. He marched with a brisk military step over to the nearest member of the sect and demanded:

"Passport!"

"We have none," he replied seraphically. "We are the twelve apostles; we don't need them."

"What's your name?" the officer shouted.

In a tone of growing ecstasy: "Matthew, I am the Apostle Matthew."

The officer grabbed him by his long hair and barked out an order. Soldiers dogtrotted onto the bus and hustled the twelve North Americans down the aisle and onto the side of the road. The lieutenant came toward me, shaking his head in disbelief. "Do you know them?"

"Never seen them before!" I replied.

"Did you hear what they told me?"

"I did."

"What am I supposed to put in my report? That I arrested the twelve Apostles because they were traveling without passports?"

I limp and lurch
down streets unknown
my pretender's identity
will cost me another dawn

The life of an accidental fugitive is exhausting.

The most nerve-racking aspect is security; you're constantly second-guessing yourself, wondering if what you're doing complies with the set of rules you established for yourself to avoid capture. As time passes, you come to understand that the more paranoid you become, the safer it makes you. Every detail of daily life becomes the focus of a hallucinatory succession of suspicions and concerns.

Acting out a reassuring-social-stereotype is already a drain, sapping your mental health. But there is more, and it's even worse.

The first rule for playing a part on the urban stage is always to convey the impression that you are on your way to some place specific. A fugitive can't afford to look as if he has time on his hands. He must walk quickly, eyes on the sidewalk ahead of him, as if in a hurry. He must travel only by public transportation. A car is far too dangerous. If he encounters a roadblock, or has even a minor fender-bender, his cover is blown. He must always remember to get rid of his bus ticket; if arrested, that ticket could give the police crucial information that might lead to his place of residence and his workplace. When traveling by train, bus, or subway, he must always study his fellow passengers to determine whether one of them is a plainclothes cop.

I was constantly noticing individuals who not only had the face of an undercover cop, but who stared at me incessantly. Probably it was because I had attracted their attention with all my discreet sidelong glances. Alarm bells ringing in my mind, I would get off at the next stop, and wait for another train or bus. Getting places took forever. If, by some coincidence, the supposed plainclothes cop got off at the same stop, I would panic, thinking to myself: "Oh, Jesus, now he's following me," and I would begin to implement extremely intricate techniques to shake off anyone who might be trying to shadow me, such as running up a down escalator, or hopping onto another train heading who-knows-where, and then hopping back off just as the doors were closing. Having seen *The French Connection* four times helped me refine this particular routine.

I would carefully explore the topography and terrain of each city I lived in, making a list of all the cafés, bars, and shops with a rear exit; I designed ideal emergency routes. If I wanted to go and buy a newspaper, before committing to the newsstand, I would walk into a café and back out again, and do the same with a pharmacy and a department store.

In big cities, you need to be careful even when walking from one place to another; the police tend to keep a close eye on central and even outlying areas, wherever large numbers of people tend to come and go. Small teams of undercover agents monitor station entrances and exits, major department stores, and chokepoints in pedestrian traffic, combing the crowds for fugitives. Not only do they check the IDs of individuals who look suspicious or act in a questionable manner, but they also make a few random stops of completely respectable-looking people. This type of unpredictable questioning was especially common in Paris, Madrid, and Barcelona, and the police were well trained and skilled at their jobs. No matter how careful I might be, I was frequently caught up in these dragnets, fortunately without any negative consequences. At the time, I didn't know that no one was actually looking for me. I placed my trust in a litany of self-protection that, with the passage of time, I came to consider increasingly effective.

"I'm a good person, I'm a good person, I'm such a good person," I would recite in my head as I walked past policemen, in an attempt to emanate positive energies. For a while, I tried to recommend the use of this mantra to others, but their response was a healthy skepticism that verged occasionally on scorn.

There were times, however, when the only safe thing to do was stay inside. A terrorist attack or an official visit by a head of state would put the representatives of the law into a state of tension and high alert that rendered impotent even my magic spells.

At times like these, I would make a strategic decision and move to some quiet out-of-the-way spot, say a small village on the Basque coast, where the Guardia Civil had abandoned even their local barracks, now a playground for the more reckless local youngsters. There I spent the most idyllic periods of my entire time as a fugitive; I would take long, relaxed strolls along the beach or in the forests. Even at times like these, however, I had regrets. I wished I was Basque, or Breton, or Corsican, or Irish. I wished I could lay claim to a larger identity—a people, a language, a tradition.

The locals were generally pretty nice, and as time passed they invited me to take part in big *fiestas*, which tended to involve serious drinking. At first, however, while treating me with unfailing courtesy, they kept me at arm's length. At the first fiesta I attended, I came with a camera; I found myself immediately surrounded by a cluster of men of all ages. They very politely relieved me of my camera, exposed the film that was in it, and only then handed it back to me. Then they asked me:

"¿Italiano?"

"Sí."

"¿Fascista?"

"¡¡No!!"

"¿Sabes que es la Ikurriña?"

"Cierto, es la bandera del pueblo de Euskadi."

"¿Te gusta?"

"¡Claro que sí, hombre!"

A glass miraculously appeared in my hand, and I stayed up late with them that first night (of many). One of our chief topics of conversation was *Ogro*, the movie that Gillo Pontecorvo made about the terrorist attack and assassination of the minister in the Franco regime, Carrero Blanco. The Basques didn't like the movie; they were offended at the conceit of a foreign director who claimed to have understood everything that happened. I had had some doubts about the movie myself, but I wasn't going to let them criticize my beloved Pontecorvo, if only because he had made *The Battle of Algiers*. We would argue for hours, sitting on benches in the square overlooking the harbor. Whenever our conversation died down, I started singing at the top of my lungs "Vuela, Carrero Blanco vuela . . . " and then we would start drinking again.

They constantly asked me to tell them about the demonstrations held by the Italian protest movement against the execution of the anarchist Salvador Puig Antich, who was garroted in the final years of Franco's dictatorship. It had become a ritual. I would stand up, I would take a cane from one of the old men, and I would begin marking out a map on the ground, explaining as I went: "We were here, the police were there, and the Spanish embassy was in the middle, right here . . . "

For years, I dreamed of moving back to this little town for good, once my troubles with the law had been resolved. I even liked the little cemetery, on a hillside midway between the sea and the mountains.

Last summer, I finally did go back, but everything had changed. The walls were covered with copies of a huge poster with an incredible number of little photographs: the faces of prisoners, new and old. The program of fiestas was devoted, by now, only to raising funds and gathering support for the campaign in favor of amnesty, and the people seemed listless, worn out by the daily effort to preserve the memory of their dream.

The romantic tranquility of the little graveyard that I had so loved was tainted by the recent death of a young man who had fallen out the window of a police station in Bilbao. The usual open window, the usual police detective who had been looking the other way.

I only stayed long enough to understand that I would never be coming back. I decided on cremation instead of burial.

The most dangerous place for a fugitive is the house where he's living. A slip up, a piece of poor judgment, or pure chance can bring it to the attention of the police. There are three possible scenarios for the ensuing arrest: in your apartment (the most dangerous time is in the early morning), at the main door as you leave, or along your route back home.

Choosing the right place to live isn't enough. You also need to know in considerable detail everything that goes on around it. This meant that once I had the keys to my new home, I spent the first week indoors, never going out, watching and making notes on everyone and everything, through the slits in my lowered blinds. Armed with a pair of binoculars, I spied on my neighbors, both in my own apartment building and in nearby buildings, as well as on the shops, the delivery men, the routine police patrols, the firemen, the private security guards and the street sweepers; recording schedules, habits, license plates, and vehicle models.

On one wall of my room, I tacked up big sheets of paper, which corresponded to sectors of the street. I wrote on them everything I saw. I would establish a "typical scenario" of what happened in the street, and then I classified it in terms of a standard number of time slots that covered a full twenty-four-hour day. This template allowed me to identify immediately any "false notes." Alarm bells would go off every time I saw someone lingering outside an apartment building doorway, a car or a delivery truck that I had never seen before, a group of repairmen hard at work, and I had to go through a complicated procedure to check them out.

If the questionable element was a delivery truck (one of the most common vehicles used in capturing fugitives, because it is an ideal platform for the conveyance of a full-fledged and self-contained surveillance structure), and it failed to leave the neighborhood in a reasonable period of time, then I'd adopt the ploy of phoning the police:

"Yes, ahem, good evening. This is Mister . . . , and I live in . . . Street. This evening, I took my dog out for a walk, just like I normally do, and I noticed that a man who had just parked a delivery truck outside of number . . . on my street got out and ran over to a waiting car. The car took off in a hurry. Um, hum, that's right. It left so fast that it screeched its tires. I think they were both Arabs."

Then I would hung up the phone, step out of the phone booth, and wait. If a patrol car arrived three minutes later, I would go back upstairs to my apartment, and make dinner. Otherwise, I would go spend the night at a friend's house.

The truly singular effect of spying on your neighbors is that it takes you into their lives; aside from their schedules and their habits, you learn lots of other things about them. People do the oddest things within the shelter of their own homes. There were times when I was drawn into genuine family dramas: married couples quarreling, parents fighting with their children, or even lovers' spats. And so it was often much more entertaining to track the saga of the family on the fifth floor than to watch television.

The thing that impressed me most was the time and energy that men and women devote to cheating on one another. I used to think that in our modern society consummating a betrayal in one's own home was something that belonged to the past. It is a perfectly normal thing, after all, to go to a hotel. But that's not the way things work. I have observed an incredible array of strategies for cheating, carried out with a cunning and cold determination that can only make us pray, devoutly, that none of these people ever takes up a life of crime.

In Mexico City, the only ironbound security rules were: avoid being noticed, to the extent that it is possible, and frequent only those neighborhoods that are compatible with your appearance and the social class that you are trying to depict. The only free zone was the university campus; there the police were forbidden entry, and campus security was the responsibility of the university's own security staff. I enrolled in school, taking classes in the history department, and I spent most of my time in that happy enclave.

Going unnoticed meant, in particular, avoiding robbery by the police. The police frequently used a routine identity check as an opportunity to demand your wallet and your watch. Not a day passed without some foreign student coming onto campus with a story about how they had been obliged to make an involuntary contribution to fatten up the meager salaries of the police force. It never happened to me because I had immediately learned to pay first. Whenever I was stopped by a cop, I would discreetly hand over one hundred pesos (the price of a Coca-Cola), and be on my way without a problem.

The most common victims were the Japanese students. That was not only because they had high-quality watches and because the exchange rate for the yen was so high, but also because of a deep-rooted and virulent hatred against the slant-eyed race in general. Around the turn of the twentieth century, hundreds of thousands of Chinese were led to flee the subhuman living conditions in their homeland with the lure of a guaranteed job in a Mexico that was about to erupt in full-fledged revolution. Some four thousand Chinese were murdered in the course of just a few years, largely because of resentment that they were taking jobs from *campesinos* who were only marginally less poor than they.

*

I lived in a little row house in the Colonia Roma neighborhood, founded by Italian emigrants and now occupied in part
by the city's Jewish community. It was a safe neighborhood,
patrolled 24-7 by vigilante-style security guards with itchy trig-
ger fingers. In fact, aside from Colonia Roma and the university campus, there weren't many other neighborhoods that I
could safely go, especially not the Zona Rosa (the downtown
tourist area) and San Angel (the quarter frequented by intellectuals and artists).

The main risk was an encounter with a gang of *panchitos*,
young men from the worst neighborhoods and the *ciudades
perdidas*, favelas that were themselves the size of an ordinary
city, and which did not officially exist. With no running water,
no sewer systems, no electricity, they are home to the poor who
have escaped from the countryside. Every so often, the *panchitos* chose a wealthy neighborhood to raid. They'd hijack a few
city buses and arrive two hundred strong, operating with military precision; while one group of the attackers provided
cover, engaging in fierce firefights with the police, the rest of
the *panchitos* looted stores.

I had only one minor brush with the *panchitos*. I was invited to a party at the home of a noted Communist labor organizer, to celebrate his sister's *quinceanera* (the most important
celebration for a Mexican woman, because it constitutes her
entry into society). The labor organizer lived near the airport,
in a quarter that might have been described as "working-class"
back in the sixties but that unemployment in the decades since
then had transformed into something indescribable. I had
gone to the party with friends, in a car, because if I had tried
to go alone, by bus, I would certainly have been beaten up.
The party was held on the large, flat roof of the house; it was
lovely and cheerful. There were professional, choreographed
dancers celebrating with the guest of honor.

Midway through the party, I ran out of cigarettes, and I asked where I could go to buy a pack in the neighborhood. There was immediately a palpable sense of tension in the air, and the other guests all began pressing their own packs of cigarettes upon me. The sight of their dignified poverty made it impossible for me to accept their gifts, and I headed for the door, ready to find a smoke shop myself; they blocked my way, in an openly friendly manner. As I usually do, I had completely misconstrued the situation; I assumed that they had taken offense at my refusal. But considering the rate I was smoking, I was afraid that I would finish off everyone else's supply. At that point, the labor organizer ordered a group of people to accompany me to buy cigarettes. There were at least fifteen guys, and they formed a moving barrier around me as we walked. I still hadn't figured out the situation, but as soon as I entered the first bar, I began to curse my weakness for cigarettes. The bar was teeming with *panchitos*, and as soon as they laid eyes on me they started negotiating with my friends to determine how much money the gringo would need to pay in order to be left in peace. The two groups faced off in the proverbial Mexican standoff, with yours truly dying of terror between them. I recovered my senses after a while, and, waving a handful of money over my head, I began to shout that it was a day of celebration and that I was happy, indeed, delighted, to pay for a round for everyone in the bar. That defused the situation, but that pack of cigarettes cost me a fortune. I was invited to other parties in that same neighborhood, but I always had unavoidable prior obligations.

In short, it was exhausting and draining to follow security rules in that deranged and bloodthirsty megalopolis. I wasn't sure how to behave in the various situations I encountered and I could never relax. I was constantly tense and wary. It was probably because I was so anxious to extricate myself from this state of incessant anxiety that I fell, plump and unsuspecting prey, into the trap of Melvin Cervera Sanchez. His courteous manners and the possibility of being reborn with a new identity made me overlook the obvious rule that when someone insists on seeing a fugitive home, no matter how inconvenient the kindly gesture, his actions are certainly not prompted by the milk of human kindness.

And yet they saw him
skating in the moonlight
singing and laughing
without making a sound

E ven though the Vatican has never acknowledged his existence, I feel certain that there is a patron saint of accidental fugitives. He's not as efficient as his patron-saintly colleagues because, like those he protects, he is forced to operate undercover. He does what he can. More than once, I have been the beneficiary of his benevolence.

One morning, in Paris, I woke up with a terrible toothache. I absolutely needed to see a dentist, and a Chilean friend let me borrow his health insurance card. I went to a public health clinic and, after filling out a number of forms, and patiently waiting my turn, I finally sat down in the dentist's chair.

I have never really thought much of dentists, but that day I loved every one of them, even the dentists that had tortured me when I was a child. Fear of the dentist's drill is an inherited trait in my family, and our dentist knows it perfectly well. Whenever one of us comes into his office, he locks the door and pockets the key to ensure that we can't escape. The wiliest patient is my brother, who has achieved the inconceivable in his efforts to avoid having a filling. Now, as soon as he enters the dentist's office, they take away his car keys and impound his shoes.

The dentist in whose hands I was placing my pain and my mouth was about thirty-five; he had a little blond goatee tacked onto an impertinent French face. He began to explore my oral cavity. Even though I kept trying to indicate the tooth that was causing the pain, mumbling explanations and pointing with my index finger, he was interested in something else in there.

"Oh, no," I thought to myself, "an idiot dentist."

But that wasn't it. In fact, he was the dentist-nephew of Sherlock Holmes.

"Are you Chilean?" he asked, as he continued to root around with his probe.

"Of course," I managed to say.

"And you had these fillings done in Chile?"

"Right."

"How long have you lived in France?"

I did my best to remember the issue date of my friend's health insurance card: "Let's see . . . um, yes, three years," I answered, pushing his hand away from my mouth.

"And have you ever lived in other countries?"

"No but, excuse me, why are you asking all these questions?" I ventured to query, in an attempt to understand what he was driving at.

"Because you aren't Chilean. Your health card is a fake or else it belongs to someone else; by now we know all the tricks that you immigrants use to exploit our health system."

This wasn't going well, and I played one of the few cards left me—indignation:

"Why how dare you? This is a perfectly valid health card. Of all things to have happen. I'm suffering from a toothache, I go to see a dentist, and instead of treating my toothache he tries to tell me I'm not Chilean. How on earth could you say such a thing?"

"These fillings were done in Europe, my dear sir, and many years ago, when you were just a child. Are you Spanish? Italian?"

"I am Chilean, how many times do I have to tell you?"

"Don't insult my intelligence," he shouted. "You're Chilean? Then tell me the word that you normally use to describe tartar in Chile."

"I can't remember," I mumbled.

"Then I'm calling the police."

I stared into the abyss. Faced with the apocalyptic prospect of winding up in prison with a toothache, I made a last-ditch attempt: "Please, don't call the police. You're right, I'm not Chilean, I'm Italian. But I'm not an immigrant, the police are looking for me. I'm facing a jail term of fifteen years if they send me back; I've already spent three years in prison. And I'm innocent. I've been charged with a crime I never committed; the whole story is a mess that I won't even bore you with. If you call the police, you'd be sending an innocent man to prison, believe me."

My heart was in my throat. All I could do was wait to see what he would do next, as I lay, tilted back in the dentist's chair, my neck wrapped in a white towel, like a gag. I stared at him in despair. Suddenly I saw a light all around him. My eyes widened in astonishment. Yes, I had seen it. Just for a second.

The saint without a name had touched his heart, and suddenly he was kindly and gentle. After administering anesthesia, he picked up the drill and used it with a delicate, almost tender touch. I felt no pain.

"You'll need to come back next week to have the medication removed; make an appointment with my nurse," he said, turning his back to me as he put his instruments away. I waited in the room for a while, trying to understand if it was a con, and I finally decided that it wasn't.

"Thanks for everything, doctor." I went back, despite the advice of all my friends, who told me in every language spoken on earth that I was crazy, and that if I went, the police would be waiting to greet me. I had an instinct that the dentist would not betray me. And I was right: nothing bad happened. In fact, he cleaned my teeth. As I was about to leave, I gave in to my curiosity:

"Listen, doctor, could you tell me something? Would any dentist have noticed?"

"No. I worked in Chile for a couple of years."

I started laughing:

"You mean to say that out of the hundreds of dentists in Paris, I ran into the only one that could cause me problems?"

He was laughing too. "That's probably right."

"So long, doctor. You're a good man."

Another time, our patron saint intervened with a taxi driver. I was with Alessandra and we had stayed out late at a party. The Metro had stopped running some time earlier and we lived on the other side of the city. As a basic security precaution, we walked about ten blocks away from our friend's house before starting to look around for a taxi. After a while we found one. I can't remember what the driver looked like, because I couldn't take my eyes off the German shepherd sitting next to the driver and eyeing us in an unsettling way.

Taxi drivers in Paris are convinced that every one of their fares is a potential mugger, and they've outfitted themselves accordingly. They travel with ferocious dogs; they carry electric cattle prods or cans of pepper spray. Urban legends tell of rear seats that trap the passenger and other diabolical gadgets. I have always been afraid of taxi drivers and, aware of the fact that I am not exactly the most fortunate person on earth—in fact, I am particularly prone to the worst kinds of trouble—I have always avoided doing anything that might make my driver suspicious. Such as putting my hand into my pocket a little too quickly, or looking around nervously.

Despite the late hour, we ran into a line of cars leading into an underpass along the Seine. A few hundred yards ahead, I could see the unmistakable lights of a police car, and I assumed that there had been an accident.

Wrong. It was one of those really nasty roadblocks, where they stopped everyone and checked everyone's documents very carefully. I might look like Gustave, but all I had in my pocket was my Italian identity card. I never would have carried it off. The minutes ticked by, and slowly but inexorably we drew closer to the police barriers blocking the road. I didn't know what to do; getting out of the cab and running was not an option. They would have caught me immediately.

I was just resigning myself to the worst when Alessandra burst into tears, weeping bitterly, which in turn caused the dog to bark and attracted the taxi driver's attention. An odd conversation sprang up between them. She in Italian, he in French, the dog in German Shepherd.

And that was when the saint placed his hand on the taxi driver's conscience and made a charitable man of him. He stepped out of the taxi and began to shout at the police: "This city is a disaster, we can never work in peace. The traffic jams during the day aren't enough already. Now the police want to block traffic at night too. I've got a family to feed. If I have to sit here all night like some jerk-off, how am I supposed to work?" His outburst caught everybody's attention. When I saw a police officer walking aggressively toward us, I sank back into my seat, doing my best to blend into the upholstery.

"What is all this noise?" demanded the *flic*. "There is a police operation going on, and citizens need to cooperate." He clearly didn't know much about Parisian taxi drivers, if he thought he could appeal to their sense of civic duty. In fact, the cab driver began to show off all his inborn talent at quarreling, and just five minutes later the police officer was throwing in the towel: "You, down there!" he yelled to the policemen manning the traffic barrier. "Move that out of the way before I arrest this pain-in-the-ass."

We drove through the checkpoint under the astonished eyes of all the other drivers. The cabbie roared through the streets like a madman until we reached the destination I'd given him, grunted his refusal of the generous tip I offered, and pulled out, tires squealing, cursing Italians and the police with equal venom.

*

When I lived in Pigalle, at my Peruvian friend's house, I used to avoid the Metro station because there was a little group of intelligent-looking undercover policemen there. I would enter and leave the neighborhood by making my way through a network of narrow lanes and winding streets lined with seedy bars and night clubs. At every corner, there were girls of all races and colors, day and night.

Everyone who lives in Pigalle knows everybody else. After awhile I became a familiar face, and no one tried to sell me cheap thrills anymore. The girls called out greetings to me whenever they saw me, and it was a source of some embarrassment. I always felt a little vulnerable and exposed, because the profession they practice endows them with a special gift for seeing through people.

One evening two pimps decided that the best thing to do with their time was to shoot one another in a bar. The one with the slow draw and the unsteady aim wound up dead on the floor, side-by-side with a chance victim, a customer who'd picked the wrong bar that night. The other pimp got away but the police were sure that he was still in the neighborhood and began a full-fledged sweep.

As seems to be practically routine with me—finding myself in the wrong place at the wrong time—I got out at Notre Dame de Lorette, two stops short of Pigalle, and I began to wend my way through the narrow streets with only one thing in mind—getting home and going to sleep. I immediately noticed that something wasn't right. The street corners were empty and the shutters of the clubs were all pulled down. Just as I walked into the Place Saint-Georges, I saw a fleet of police vans from the Gendarmerie coming up behind me.

I started walking faster, but by the time I reached the Rue Condorcet I saw some men in dark-blue uniforms coming toward me and stopping everyone they met. I turned on my heel and started looking around for an unguarded cross street to dart down when I saw one of the girls opening the street door of an apartment building.

I walked over to her: "Let me in, please!"

"I'm not working tonight," she said, and closed the door in my face.

But the patron saint of fugitives whispered in her ear that that was a day for good deeds, and a few seconds later she opened the door again. "What do you want?" she asked.

"There's a police sweep, I don't have my documents, and I don't want to be arrested. Please, please let me in."

She read the fear on my face: "All right, come on in."

I followed her to a studio apartment that reeked vaguely of humanity and stale smoke. "This is where I work; I live in Clignancourt. You live in the neighborhood, don't you?"

I smiled at her, I offered her a cigarette, but didn't say a word. Shaking her head, she said: "I didn't mean to be nosy."

"And I didn't mean to be rude," I answered. "Thanks for the hospitality, but I'd rather talk about generalities."

"Hey, you know, everybody here knows that I'm a girl you can trust. Felix cares about those things."

"Who's Felix?" I asked.

"My man."

"Would he get mad if he came in and found me here?"

"No, he never comes in here. He never leaves the bar, except to go to sleep."

"By the way, why is the police out in force tonight?"

"Two assholes shot each other in a bar. I don't know exactly what happened; the cops showed up and I scrammed. I hope Felix doesn't get in trouble. He's already been in prison twice."

"Is he your pimp?"

"Yes."

That was all we had to say to one another, and we spent the rest of the time smoking cigarettes and looking at our watches.

When "radio Pigalle" reported that the alert was over and the shooter had been arrested, I thanked her and went home. From that day on, I greeted the girls without embarrassment, and every so often my savior would stop me and ask me to give her a cigarette.

Sometimes though,
maybe because I'm young
I have no reason why

I never really know what to say when someone asks me what my everyday life on the run was like. Whenever I could, I worked—in Mexico I even enrolled in the university—but the main focus of my days was food. And in fact I was a bulimic fugitive.

I immediately developed a compulsive eating disorder, bulimia, and after just a couple of months I had already gained about sixty-five pounds. *Bernard el gordo* (Fat Bernard) is what my South American friends called me.

My bulimia came in the aftermath of an old trauma. In August of 1977 the Italian special prisons had just been inaugurated; because the bureaucracy of the penitentiary system was unable to distinguish between Lotta Continua and the Red Brigades, they decided that I was a dangerous terrorist, a menace to society, and sent me to the "superprison" in Cuneo. I was one of the first twenty "new arrivals." They locked us up in a huge room and, one at a time, clubbed us bloody. I lived in a constant state of terror. Every morning at five they would take one of us away, down into a basement room, and beat him bloody all over again.

The purpose behind this treatment was to strip us of all vestiges of human dignity, in order to create the conditions most favorable for ratting out the others. It was impossible to sleep. At night they would walk through the cell block, doing the head count, shining a spotlight in our faces each time they passed. By day, they kept the radio and the television turned on, with the volume as high as possible. When the mess cart came through, the guards would dare us to eat, assuring us they had just pissed in the food. The weekly shower offered them a chance to play hilarious pranks. One of their favorite tricks was to let us get all soaped up and then turn off the water, announcing that our allotted shower time had expired. The visiting hall seemed felt like a giant fish bowl; I had to meet my family locked up in a bulletproof glass cage. Our conversations were recorded.

We decided to rebel. And we succeeded—despite the thousand obstacles thrown in our path—in establishing a constructive debate with the inmates of the other "special prisons" scattered across Italy. The delegation of inmates held in the "kamp" of Favignana was in favor of suicide, others advocated open revolt. We decided to start an all-out hunger strike, and the others followed our lead. After we refused all food for ten days, drinking only water, the warden decided to negotiate. We managed to obtain a few minor concessions from the prison board, and in particular, a promise that there would be no more beatings.

I was the youngest, and I experienced those days of desperate struggle as a living nightmare. I suddenly began to devour food like a crazy man; I didn't stop until they transferred me to a "normal" prison.

During my life on the run, my uncontrollable obesity did give an extra dimension of credibility to my characters. And that was my standard argument whenever my girlfriend would lower the discussion to the mere plane of physical attraction.

"Why don't you pretend you're a cop," I would say to her, "and you're trying to decide which of two people to stop and question. One of them is slender, athletic, and vigorous, and the other one looks like Oliver Hardy: which one would you stop?" I gradually won her over, and when we were in bed together, she would call me "my little quarter-ton."

It wasn't until the end of my time in Mexico that I managed to lose some weight. Aside from the poor quality of the food and the beverages, I was deeply shaken by the poverty and the ancestral hunger that afflicted more than half the population there. If I went out into the street to buy food at the butchers or to have something to eat in a restaurant, the sight of all that suffering, starving humanity left me without appetite, and most of the time the money I had planned to spend on the pleasures of my gullet would end up dropping into those grimy, perennially outstretched hands. My sense of guilt at being a gringo was more effective than any Weight Watchers program.

When I got back to Italy and the national prison system, my bulimia returned with a vengeance, and it ravaged my metabolism.

"The fats in his circulatory system are roughly equivalent to 400 grams of butter per liter of blood," my lawyers would thunder at press conferences and during the hearings of the Supervisory Court that had to decide on my request for release on account of poor health. The prison authorities were also in favor of a conditional release, probably encouraged in that direction by the fact that I constantly carried under one arm a copy of the book, *A History of Cannibalism in Europe*.

During that period, I wasn't the only one worrying the warden. A fellow Paduan, imprisoned for armed robbery, decided that he didn't want to spend any more time in prison. He decided that his way out was neither through the courts nor by escaping. He wanted them to kick him out of jail, and he succeeded. He would shuffle around the prison wearing a red plastic colander on his head, eyes cast downward, taking short, nervous steps. In one hand he carried a rectangular piece of cardboard, with "KGB identity card" written in large, clear letters. Every day, for months, he managed to make his way into the offices of the warden, the Carabiniere commander, the registry office, the chaplain, and the prison physician, asking them all, "Has the order for my transfer to Moscow come in yet?"

They did everything they could to get rid of him, but his reputation had spread through the prison system and all the other penitentiaries refused to accept him as a prisoner. They tried to cajole him, bribe him, they even tried beating him, but he toughed it out. In the end, in total exasperation, they got rid of him by having a doctor issue a scientific finding that he was incompatible with the prison environment.

And he stayed in character right up to the end. As he walked past the last guard opening the last gate that stood between him and freedom, red colander still on his head, he held up his identity card as a secret agent and whispered: "I'm on a mission for the KGB."

If you have to become bulimic, Paris is the right place for it. Age-old culinary wisdom teaches the importance of quality in quantity. I grasped this fundamental concept immediately: I learned to dine in the right places and to avoid places like McDonald's. With a careful cross-referenced exploration of a number of tour and culinary guides, I soon narrowed down my selections to the best that the market had to offer.

I started my days with a magnificent breakfast in a pastry shop not far from the Boulevard des Italiens: a lukewarm cappuccino sprinkled with cocoa powder and sugar, followed by three cream-filled brioches, and a glass of Perrier to cleanse my palate before I sank my delicate little dessert spoon into an exquisite kiwi mousse. Around mid-morning, I would head over to the Rue de Rivoli, where there was a bistro that proffered a Côtes du Rhône and a paté de foie gras worthy of the names. At lunchtime, unless I was eating at home, I could select from a vast array of brasseries, depending on the whims of the day. My afternoon snack, usually consisting of a sandwich (you shouldn't overdo it with the sugar), was usually consumed in the neighborhood around the Madeleine, where there was an Alsatian who was a master of the difficult art of coordinating and balancing the type of bread, sauce, and meat. I would give the guy four stars for his beers as well.

Choosing the restaurant for my evening meal was generally the cause of some anxiety, so I started to consider my options from early morning. I tended to prefer French regional restaurants, but I couldn't allow myself to neglect the canon of gastronomic internationalism, which demanded frequent encounters with exotic cultures. I devoted a couple of evenings every week to that pursuit, by geographic zone: Chinese, Vietnamese, Thai, Indian, Pakistani, Afghan, Cuban, Mexican, Argentine, and so on.

One of the fundamental security rules for a fugitive is never to frequent the same restaurants; I followed that rule only for restaurants where the food was disappointing. I feel certain that the rule applies only to skinny fugitives. An obese customer who eats like a wolf is definitely not one that a restaurateur would risk losing.

Since I couldn't eat in a restaurant every day, and because I was developing an increasingly discerning palate, I learned to cook. Before I became a fugitive, my mother had done all the cooking (she was a talented and versatile cook); in culinary terms, on the other hand, my time with the Boy Scouts had taught me only how to make pasta and grill sausages.

I decided to take a scientific approach. I began by studying the sacred texts, and then explored the various schools of culinary thought (I became a bitter adversary of nouvelle cuisine, primarily because of the tiny portions); once I had equipped myself with the necessary utensils, I began to create casseroles, roasts, stews, and pastries. To serve at least four. I couldn't help it if the recipes unfailingly listed quantities of ingredients sufficient to feed from four to six persons, and once I had cooked it, I couldn't throw all that good food away. Security considerations generally kept me from inviting my friends over to my house for dinner and so, unless Alessandra was visiting me, I usually sat down to dinner alone. And, to tell the truth, my friends invited me to dinner only rarely; when they did, they would ask me to contribute some money. All things considered, they preferred to get together at a restaurant, where everybody paid their own check. When you're fat, you tend to become the butt of jokes like "I'd rather buy you a new suit than treat you to dinner," and other oh-so-funny witticisms.

I would spend three or four hours a day preparing dishes intended to delight my palate and placate my insatiable appetite. Some days I would spend the entire morning in the finest food stores shopping for the right ingredients. I spent nearly half of every Sunday rolling out the pasta dough for tortelli, ravioli, and cappellacci. I also set the table with care, from the tablecloth to the glasses and silverware. Since I have always found flowers depressing, instead of the more conventional vase of flowers, I had a centerpiece that consisted of a little doll figure of Popeye's bulimic buddy, Wimpy.

I graduated to culinary adulthood by creating my own recipes, testing them over and over before adding them to my own personal cookbook, and giving them names that sprang from various personages and episodes of my own judicial soap opera. I have no intention of printing them in this book. I've spent enough time in jail already.

I had been born into a culture of fine wine, so it wasn't much of a leap for me to begin exploring the magical enological realm of France. Every meal was unfailingly irrigated with excellent wines; I never drank to excess, always limiting myself to a reasonable proportion with the quantity of food. Sufficient wine for six guests, never more. And to top it off, I never denied myself a good cognac or a calvados.

My digestion was a thorny problem at first. The tension of living in hiding was constantly giving me heartburn and bloating. But I soon figured out a remedy. The ideal way to ensure a healthy digestion is to go to the movies. The movie house is a place of truce, a non-combat area where, once the lights are dimmed and the film is running, the only reality is the movie itself. All the little realities of the individuals in the audience are canceled.

Choosing what movie to see wasn't much of an issue; I would just go to the nearest theater. I watched a freakish number of unbelievably bad movies; some of the really bad ones I would sit through more than once. I watched a Norwegian horror-crime flick three times. (The *elevator* did it.)

When I stayed home, I would make myself comfortable in front of the television set, a bottle of hard liquor and a pack of cigarettes within easy reach. And to top things off, in the complicated equilibrium of my bulimia, smoking soon took on a crucial role: it filled in the intervals between one feeding and the next.

A fugitive, a bulimic, and a nicotine addict.

The most painful period in terms of the quality of the cuisine was certainly the time I spent as José. Confined to that horrible neighborhood by security concerns, my bulimia was obliged to settle for a sharp step down from the customary refined flavors and ingredients. It had to make do with couscous, merguez, and cheap Algerian wine.

Nowadays bulimia is fashionable. The mass media feature it frequently, and theories swarm like flies. I'm not trying to boast, here, but ten years ago I had already reached the conclusion that the overweight sector of the population is oppressed and under attack. The skinnier segment of the population cannot tolerate the diversity of their heftier fellow-humans, and live for nothing so much as to force the chunky among us to slim down.

Thin people are crafty and relentless. First of all, not only do thin people have all the diets known to man at their fingertips, but they have always developed a diet of their own, which they try to foist off on every fatty they meet. And if a thin person encounters an unreceptive fat person, he is capable of anything. The thin know how to shift at lightning speed from the soft-sell to outright threats.

In desperate cases, thin-man dietologists turn into shrinks. With the same professional tone they use to recommend breakfasts of coffee with Nutrasweet, Bulgarian yogurt, and whole-wheat zwieback toast (never more than two pieces), they start accusing the unfortunate fatty of having "problems." Unresolved relationships with his elementary school teacher or with the milkman, anxieties, insecurities, complexes—anything can be used as a weapon, a tool in the campaign to demonize the extra layer of adipose tissue of the unfortunate target of their diatribe. (All this in the distant hope that the fatty will remember their words just as he's biting into a fragrant cream-filled puff pastry, and that he'll choke on it as he is furrowing his brow in the effort to unearth, once and for all, every last issue left unresolved in connection with the milkman).

Now, if even this last-ditch effort fails, matters become still more dire. It will be necessary to dig deeper, until we identify the roots of that unholy appetite. Inevitably, the skinny guy will manage to discover, buried deep in all the fat, a death wish. This marks the beginning of the "you're trying to hurt yourself" and "this is attempted suicide, you know that don't you?" phase. Every bite of puff pastry is just another step closer to death. When confronted with a really stubborn case, the skinny guy, self-anointed dietician and psychiatrist, will quickly reveal his third specialty—cardiologist and internist. He will produce a list, worthy of a medical encyclopedia, of the forms of damage caused by triglicerides and cholesterol, and he will then proceed to a solemn description of the symptoms and course of various cardiovascular diseases. Culminating, of course, in death.

The fat man who hears all this is frightened, of course. He thinks he can feel the first pains in his chest, he envisions himself in a wheelchair, stricken with a devastating paralysis and . . . he gets hungry! He can't wait to get rid of this peevish party-pooper so that he can relax and chow down on a nice puff pastry. And if the fatty is also a smoker, the skinny guy will skip all the preliminaries and talk only about death, as if there were only minutes to go.

In any case, my weight problem immediately became a subject of discussion and concern, and after a while everybody was bothering me about it. All the same, I could consider myself fortunate: I didn't have any unresolved issues with the milkman. There was no question about the cause of my bulimia.

I have had to defend myself against skinny folk for many long years now. With any means necessary. I have gone so far as to lie, to eat and smoke in secret. Sometimes, at night, when everyone else is asleep. I have had to stop frequenting people who had managed to extort the promise that I would go on a diet, "starting next Monday . . ."

Unfortunately, my bulimia also tended to produce symptoms of gout, making me a fugitive who was both overweight and lame. Whenever that happened, I became a man on the run from my well-meaning friends as well. Gout is a disease that runs a slow and painful course; all I needed was somebody lecturing me about it.

In Mexico City, I met another bulimic. He was a Guatemalan singer-songwriter. The military death squads had tortured and murdered his whole family. He no longer sang, but he carried his guitar with him everywhere he went. Some Mexican artists

I knew had played me tapes of a few of his old concerts; I have to say, he was really good.

I would run into him often at friends' houses, sitting in a chair, his guitar resting on his knees, his hands slowly but systematically lifting food to his mouth. I would always sit next to him; together we looked like a pair of characters out of a Botero painting. People assumed that we were close friends, as they saw us talking in quiet undertones for hours at a time.

With roughly the same passion as a pair of junkies remembering a trip taken years ago to the Golden Triangle, we would talk about food. We would recount to one another family lunches and dinners, the smells, the flavors, and the atmosphere from times when we had been happy.

He died in 1990 in a forest in northern Guatemala, near the Mexican border. He died fighting. He had set aside his guitar and joined the ranks of the guerrillas who were defending the Indios from genocide.

In Paris, the exile community had long ago grasped the scale of the psychic and physical devastation caused by exile, torture, and imprisonment. The struggle to keep from crossing over the razor thin barrier dividing psychological discomfort from full-blown pathology was a very common problem in their circles.

The South American community in Paris, in particular, was ravaged by suicides and alcoholism. The intellectual class was able to fit into this alien society and, albeit with great difficulty, to overcome their traumas. But the Indios, with ancestral ties to their land, whether they were *mineros* or *campesinos*, experienced their state of exile as if they had been herded onto a reservation.

The debate caught the interest of a great many people; an extensive and articulated medical and human support network was created for those who fell ill, and I turned to that network more than once. Each community had cases of its own, but everyone knew about them through a sort of transverse jungle telegraph that served as a sort of medical update. One of the best known cases was that of my friend Lolo.

Lolo was Chilean. His real name was Jorge. Jorge Saball Astaburuaga. The son of Catalonian anarchists who fled Spain after Franco's victory, he had grown up in the Chilean left wing, working as an activist in the ranks of the United Popular Action Movement (Movimiento de Acción Popular Unitario—MAPU). He was clear-eyed and ironic, free of ideological hobgoblins, probably because of the rich mix of libertarian blood flowing in his veins.

The day of the anti-Allende coup, September 11, 1973, his father pulled an old German pistol out of a trunk—a relic of the Spanish Civil War—and handed it to him, urging him to escape. He was eighteen years old. There were road blocks everywhere in Santiago. Lolo and a friend of his, a policeman who had remained loyal to Allende, decided to take their fate into their own hands when they found themselves looking down yet another road with a checkpoint. They were separated in the firefight. Lolo made it to Paris still certain that his friend had died in the exchange of fire. He was wrong: his comrade had managed to survive and had gone into exile in Rome. For years, they mourned one another reciprocally, until they met again during a conference of Chilean exiles in Frankfurt.

In the meantime, Lolo had already contracted cancer. The horrors of the Pinochet regime lived on in his body in the form of a tumor that was gradually eating him alive. Chilean exiles all over Europe knew about Lolo and his cancer. He had become a symbol of their suffering. And of their resistance. It seemed as if he had no purpose in life other than politics, enjoying the beauty of music, his relationship with his partner in life, Vicky, and his friendships. I was one of those friends. He protected me and coddled me, between operations and cycles of chemotherapy. He taught me the secret of self-deprecating humor as a way of warding off the brutality of life, and he taught me to love music. He always used to tell me that I was a young barbarian. And he was certainly right about that. In fact, my musical appreciation was limited to songs I'd learned in the Boy Scouts or in the protest movement. I would go to see him, and he would have me listen to one record after another, leading me by the hand through the world of great music.

He was the last person I saw before leaving Paris. He arrived late and out of breath, just in time to give me the last cassette he had made for me. I never saw him again. After I returned to Italy, Lolo was one of the founders and one of the most active members of the "Comité International Justice pour Massimo Carlotto."

In that period, the first cracks in the wall of the Pinochet dictatorship were allowing many exiles to return to Chile. Lolo was one of those who could have gone home immediately. But he stayed in Paris for a long time to work for the Comité. When he left, it was already too late. He only had time to make it back to Chile and realize that the cancer had unleashed its final, victorious offensive.

Checho, a close friend to both of us, kept me posted on his lingering agony; one day he told me that he would soon slip into a coma and that this was my last chance to to bid him farewell. I called him on the phone, but when I heard his voice, distant and a little remote, I could think of nothing to say but banalities. Afterwards, I wept with shame at having failed to express to him what I truly felt.

He died in slow motion. Vicky, Checho, and other comrades stayed with him until the end, for every minute of his death throes. They held his hand; he would squeeze their fingers from time to time to show that he was still there. They washed him and made sure his headphones were in place and the tape recorder was still working. Lolo wanted die in the company of his beloved music.

He died listening to the Italian singer-songwriter, Francesco De Gregori. The news of his death was reported around the world. It was December 2, 1991. Everyone who could went back to Santiago to bid him farewell.

Checho eulogized Lolo at a gathering of hundreds, and scattered his ashes in the square while street musicians, shivering with grief, performed *Viatge a Itaca* by the Catalonian songwriter Lluís Llach: " . . . Buen viaje a los guerreros si a son pueblo son fieles, el velamen de su bajel favorezca el dios de los vientos." A short while later, I received a transcript of Checho's eulogy, with a letter from Lolo's parents.

"Dear Lolo, I have the unhappy task of bidding you a last farewell. We know that if by some miracle you were able to see us and hear us, you would just scoff at us, because ceremonies, speeches, and commemorations were so distant from your way of thinking and the essence of who you were. But that doesn't matter. These words are for you, but they are for us too . . . "

I, too, believe that that day Lolo must have been bored, and he probably told everyone to go fuck themselves, in a spectral voice. Whenever we talked about it, he would say that death is no reason to be in a bad mood.

When he was in exile, he had abandoned the MAPU and embraced once and for all anarchy. He detested every aspect of Communist "ceremonial," but the Communists loved Lolo and, in respect for diversity, they commemorated him as well.

As a child of the Seventies, I grew up thinking that death could be as light as a feather or as heavy as a mountain. Lolo's death sailed over the rooftop of the world.

He stayed in France for me, despite his love for his homeland. He burnt up his last living energy crying out to the world that I was innocent. And now I can only wonder if my cause was worth it. I know what he would have said, but it's not enough to chase away the sadness.

*

Exile, the torment of homesickness, the desperate longing to return to one's homeland, death.

Lolo returned home and died surrounded by the love of friends and family. Other exiles were less fortunate, and still others went home knowing that death awaited them. Other sharp-peaked mountains, marking a savage border between our hearts and our memories. First Tomás. Then Xavier, shot down in the front door of his house. He had failed to understood that it was not yet time to go back to Honduras. Belinda, my Peruvian friend from Pigalle, who died while fighting in the ranks of Tupac Amaru. And Carmen the nurse, killed by a mortar shell in El Salvador, together with the two children that she was hurrying to safety. Rumpled letters, carried in too many pockets, or voices distorted by the weird echoes of intercontinental phone calls: a date, the cause of death. But it is the why that tends to elude me. The why behind those decisions, decisions that ripened in exile. Decisions that were so terrible, so courageous, and perhaps so terribly mistaken. I suspect that often those decisions were dictated by the destiny of mere survival, the fact that they had reached safety over roads paved with blood, torture, jail, errors, and betrayals. To go back, perhaps, was the only way of settling accounts with the past. I can't say anything more. I prefer to remember them the way they were in Paris, when they called me "el gordo" and taught me how to face life with dignity.

Back then, I thought that we would all meet again someday, free and happy. It seemed that the tribute that this generation of third-world revolutionaries had paid to history was already overwhelming. I miss them terribly. I know that someday I will go to the plaza in Santiago where Lolo's ashes were scattered, and I will see them all again. Someday.

On the brink of the abyss
you grasp at words
but they have nothing to do with you
they speak for themselves

A ll things considered, the routine of life on the run in Europe was an unhurried delirium. In the bits of free time left to me, when I wasn't working to gratify my insatiable appetite, I tried to do something with "meaning," such as work, for instance. They were always jobs that were subcontracted, officially attributed to someone else. Most of the time, I did translations, an activity that allowed me to stay home and earn a decent living. For a long time, I translated Italian photonovellas into French. It was fun but exhausting; I was paid two francs a frame, and I basically had to invent every word of it, because all I got was a brief summary of the plot. Once I realized that no one checked my work, I started "slipping in" social and political messages here and there, at first very cautiously, but later, on a grand scale, since it was evident that the publisher never received complaints or objections. I think I reached the high point of daring when I had the heroine of the series express profound sorrow over the death of Andropov and equally keen disappointment over the election of Chernenko.

To keep from upsetting the flow of the heartwrenching love stories, I only toyed with the pictures in which people were either meeting or saying goodbye. For instance, instead of: "Hello, Gino, how is your grandmother doing?" — "Oh, she's fine, she just has a slight cold . . ." I would put: "Hello, Gino, what does your grandmother think about the strike over at the Renault plant?" — "Oh, she thinks it's generally a good thing, though she has her doubts about the platform of demands put forward by the CGT."

Admittedly, these additions did little or nothing for the characters, who, on close reading, seemed like mental cases given to fugue states, and probably socially dangerous. But most readers of photonovellas are primarily interested in only one thing: a happy ending.

I also typed theses or worked as a research assistant. I spent a lot of time finding research material in libraries.

For ten days I even worked as a waiter in an Italian pizzeria in Madrid. It wasn't a bad place to work, though I sort of resented the fact that the restaurant staff had to be satisfied with just a pizza for dinner. The Moroccan pizza chef had it in for me though, because he said that I had taken a job that should rightly have gone to one of his cousins. All my order tickets went right to the bottom of the pile, and my customers expressed their irritation at the resulting delays by forgetting to leave a tip. I knew that if I stayed on, this would end in an argument, a fight, and who knows what other trouble, so I quit and went in search of another job.

If I had had to depend on my earnings, I would have lived in dire poverty. Luckily, my parents were very generous. I felt a burden of guilt at not being able to fend for myself, but the life of an accidental fugitive is expensive. Whenever I was forced to move, I would lose my security deposit, all my furniture, and my various household objects, and that meant that I had to buy new things for the house. Each of my characters had a wardrobe of his own, and I always needed to have at least one fall-back suit of clothes, for emergencies. And last of all, I always needed to have a substantial sum of money on hand so that I would be able to leave whatever country I was in at a moment's notice.

From this point of view, I had an enviable situation compared with most of the exiles and refugees living in Europe in those years. Despite the solidarity of all the exiled comrades, making ends meet wasn't easy. If you didn't have specific professional skills, such as a degree in medicine, then you had to make do with the first job that came along. Even back then life was expensive, rents were high, and apartments were hard to find. I lived for a number of months in a rat hole in the Place de la République; there were many others who did that for years at a time.

The Italian community in Paris had the hardest time. I never had anything to do with them because they were all suspected of being terrorists and were therefore closely monitored, both by the French and the Italian police. Other exiles, from other communities, would bring me reports about them. They strongly recommended that I steer clear of them. A number of the Italians, they told me, were collaborating with the Sûreté, informing on their own community, in exchange for assurances that they would not be sent back to Italy. I never gave much credence to that rumor, though, and in fact in all these years I have never found any substantiation of it.

In part, the Italians were genuine victims of political persecution, and in the end they were allowed to return home. In other cases, the homesickness for Italy was so overwhelming that they were willing to serve their time in prison rather than spend the rest of their lives in exile. A substantial number of them still live in Paris, or in who knows what other remote part of the world, waiting for their country to close the book on the Seventies, once and for all.

Recently, one of them died. He was a lawyer, he was fifty-seven years old, and he was waiting for the statute of limitations to run out on the crimes he was accused of, so that he could go back to Italy. I read he died of a heart attack. That's not true. Exile killed him. He wasn't the first and, unfortunately, he is not likely to be the last. Someone who is twenty years old today knows little or nothing about that period. Those who are older, unless they lived in direct contact with what happened, have forgotten. Certainly, aside from friends and family members, no one remembers their names, no one remembers the story of their troubles with the law.

At the beginning of my life on the run, I had no idea of just what it meant to live as an expat. I looked around me and I didn't understand what I was seeing. The first job that I found was as a research assistant on a major history of political exile in France. In particular, I was supposed to find information in the French National Archives, focusing on documentation gathered by the Ministry of Internal Affairs. As I sat there reading those files, the personal dossiers and the police reports on a century of political asylum-seekers, it finally dawned on me what this all was. It sent a shiver of fear up my back. It was a prison without walls.

Even though I had a relatively stimulating social life, I spent most of my time alone. But work was the best way of staving off the loneliness that logistical considerations and security concerns imposed upon me.

I had made a promise to myself during the very first few days of my life on the run: "No matter what, hold out." It meant: "Abuse yourself as needed, but never give in to the temptation to surrender."

That temptation always lurks in the sheer human cost of this sort of life. I was perfectly aware of what I was doing "to myself." That is, I was aware that I had set a self-destructive mechanism in motion, but it was the only tool available to me to keep my despair from sapping what strength I could muster, the strength to keep on going, the strength to pursue that choice of freedom.

If I had simply agreed to serve out my time in prison, doing whatever I could to shorten the sentence, it would have been the smartest thing I could do in terms of the future of my own life. It would however have meant lending my endorsement to the legitimacy of the verdict and sentence issued against me. Instead, I opted for a gesture of complete rejection—flight, escape—to make an unmistakable distinction between truth and lie, justice and injustice, the law and blatant abuse of power.

I used any means necessary. When the bulimia was no longer enough to deaden my despair and my anguish was building up to the threshold of a scream—after which, of course, would come surrender—I began to activate a series of defenses to neutralize the impulse. I had identified two types of dangerous crises, which I described as "street crisis" and "home crisis."

The former was the most worrisome, because it took hold of me in full public view. I had learned to recognize the symptoms of an onset: a growing feeling of insecurity and anxiety, rising like a deep, dark tide. My footsteps became hesitant, I began to sweat profusely, and I felt a growing impulse to let myself go and drop into a dead faint. The first time this happened was in a restaurant, and when I fell, I broke a wrist. Fortunately, I was eating with friends, and they handled matters admirably.

After my wrist had been set and a cast applied, they took me to see a Turkish doctor who worked with refugees. He told me that I needed a daily cocktail of tranquilizers, antidepressants, and anti-hypertensives. That wouldn't be possible and I told him why. In order to keep my bulimia in a state of equilibrium I needed to self-administer a substantial dose of alcoholic beverages. If I mixed that with psychoactive drugs, it would slow down my response time and deaden my instincts. As a fugitive, I couldn't afford that.

And so he decided to prescribe only anti-hypertensives for me, and over the course of a number of sessions, taught me to recognize and resist these panic attacks with forms of relaxation that involved breathing techniques. That way, whenever I sensed the premonitory signs of an onset, I managed to contain the crisis and hurry home. Once I got there, I was invariably exhausted and I would drop onto my bed like a limp rag and lay there for endless hours.

The "home crisis" was not as dangerous, but much harder to overcome. Loneliness triggered it. Every once in a while, despite my rigid scheduling of the day's activities, my mind would wriggle off its leash and begin rooting around in homesickness. Every day it would get a little worse, a little more piercing. I longed for my family. The breathing technique was not a sufficiently powerful remedy. So I decided to make use of a technique I had used when I was in solitary confinement.

Between pretrial isolation and punishments, I had spent almost eight months in solitary confinement, and I learned a way of defending myself from all that useless cruelty by taking a little stroll in the world of madness: I would pretend to be a lawyer. On the table in my cell (if I had one) or on my cot, I would lay out eight objects, each of which corresponded to a judge of the Court. I would assume the role of my own defense lawyer, and I would deliver a summation for the defense that would last for hours and hours, a fiery and passionate piece of oratory, an impeccably logical exhortation. I would go on until I collapsed from sheer physical exhaustion. Then, my mind completely voided, I would drop into a troubled but restorative sleep.

During my life on the run, whenever I got to the point that I knew I just couldn't take it anymore, I would pull out a newspaper clipping with a photograph of the Appeals Court in Venice that had found me guilty. Then, after hanging it on a wall and donning an imaginary black lawyer's gown, I would begin my summation with the following words: "Most illustrious Presiding Judge, eminent judges of the Court, Esteemed

Magistrates and Jury Members, fate and God's will have placed in my hands the task of proving to you the innocence of this unfortunate young man, whose sole error has been to trust in justice . . . "

Since I knew the record of my trial by heart, I was able to develop my summations in a "professionally" credible manner. They were often so long that my panic attack would be over well before my exposition of the arguments for the defense. And so I would bring my diatribe to a close with these words: "I therefore respectfully beg this most illustrious court to adjourn the present hearing to some later date, because the effort of this daunting task has exhausted the physical strength of this advocate for the defense." And with the onset of the next attack, I would resume my summation, taking up where the court had adjourned the session.

It was a stroll through a landscape of pure madness, but as I said, any means was acceptable if it allowed me to hold out.

The "home crisis" had a variant that would manifest itself whenever I had to move. Since I couldn't call a moving company, I was forced to leave behind everything I couldn't carry with me. I went out the door one morning, never to return. These were always painful moments of extreme anguish because, more than any other time, I was forced to see clearly how makeshift and transient my life had become.

I always did my best not to become too fond of the place I happened to be living and the objects that inhabited that space, but I could hardly help it. After all, it was the only place I could feel safe, thanks to the painstaking security precautions that I took. More than that even, it was the only place I could be myself again, at least mentally.

A new place to live was a leap into the void. Was it safe? What were the neighbors like? Would my cover hold up?

The night before the move, the crisis would set in. Sleepless, I would wander from room to room, opening drawers, touching objects that I was about to lose forever, running my hands over the walls that had housed me and protected me. For the last time, I wore the clothing of a character who would be dead by sun-up, and I experienced something verging on mourning, because a "mask," "behind" which I had laughed, wept, talked, listened, and made love, would be exiting my life for good. The idea of the "new" character or the "new" house terrified me. Morning would come, and I would be sitting on the bed, still wearing my old costume, my arms wrapped figuratively around everything that I was abandoning, unable to bring myself to face the new.

Occasionally I would remain in that state for days at a time, until my friends, worried at my disappearance, would show up, reassure me, and take care of the short-term, immediate problems of the actual move for me.

The thing I hated most about moving was having to buy everything all over again; all the household objects, from furniture to silverware, that you find in any home. Normally, you buy them with the idea that they are going to last over time, be part of your everyday life, and have a history. For a fugitive, it's different: the only criterion is temporary use, and so each and every object necessarily loses its worth. I thought of them as non-objects, the non-possessions of a non-person living a non-life.

This transience of my everyday life was so painful to me that, when I left for Mexico, my mother went to the house that I had lived in as Jason and took a wooden bookcase that I had there. She took it back to Italy with her so that there would be something left from that period of my life. Now it's in my bedroom. Even though it is just a piece of cheap furniture, just a set of shelves that can be easily disassembled, I will keep it with me wherever I go, every time I move.

In other words, it wasn't easy to live from one day to another without the least prospect of a future, except for the virtual certainty that I would be going back to prison someday.

Time passed, and my presence in Europe, with its modern and efficient police forces, endowed with well-organized archives, fingerprint files, and interconnected terminals, became increasingly freighted with danger for me and for those who were helping me. The third world, with its vast spaces and its enormous contradictions, was beginning to look to me like the only possible destination: a place where I could at least formulate a hypothesis of a life.

My friends didn't want me to leave Europe. They were afraid I was too fragile, both physically and psychologically, to risk such an adventure. When I explained to them that I couldn't stand to put them in danger with my presence any longer, they told me that that was their problem, and that I needed to focus on holding out until things improved. I was certainly tempted to stay in Europe, and I had a pretty clear foreboding that the third world would wind up screwing me, but in fairness I couldn't say that I had an alternative.

Leaving my friends was heartrending. I met them, one at a time, in the street, a farewell gift, a hug, a terrible struggle to remain indifferent.

The time came to bid my family farewell, too. They had come to visit me in Paris many times before. In terms of security, it was an absurd risk, but we couldn't stay away from one another, we couldn't stand only to talk over the phone. We needed to be close together, to share an everyday life that was normal and untroubled, at least in appearance.

Our family has always been very close and the separation caused by my life on the run was a wound that would never heal in our life as a family. We experienced many trying moments in those eighteen years, but perhaps the period when I was on the run was the worst. When I was in prison, we were separated as well, but it was a different form of suffering, mitigated by daily letters and weekly visits.

Whenever they arrived in Paris, I would strip off my costumes and set aside my characters. I became a son and a brother once again. I didn't want my family to understand what I had been forced to do to myself in order to preserve my freedom. I moved out of my apartment while they were in town, and we all moved into a larger place, lent by a friend, where we all lived together. Our time together was like a holiday; we would travel around Paris, touring museums, art galleries, and monuments; we even took a ride on the Seine in a *bateau-mouche*. We would dine out, but the thing we loved best was to spend hours at the dinner table in our apartment, just talking. Tasting my mother's cooking again was always a deeply moving experience for me. In those days, we managed to heal the pain of separation and of the trials with the simple pleasure of spending time together.

The first time that they came to stay with me, I spent days on end quaking with terror at the idea of behaving like a tourist instead of a fugitive. Then I thought it over carefully and, through an exceedingly complex process of reasoning, I managed to persuade myself that I would be in absolutely no danger when I was in the company of my family. During subsequent visits I found myself behaving as if we were all invisible. And probably we really were, because we did things that were completely unthinkable for a fugitive, like spending a whole afternoon at the Centre Pompidou during a holiday weekend, surrounded by Italian tourists, or sunning ourselves high atop Notre Dame cathedral, or even spending a few hours chatting idly as we looked out over the city from the top of the Eiffel Tower.

That, in fact, was where I told my parents about my decision to leave Europe. They both fell silent, and I watched as their faces changed expression. This was the moment that we had all been dreading: being separated for good. Until then, we hadn't talked about it, but we had all known that the day would come when I would need to put the greatest possible distance between my past and my future. And that meant breaking off relations with my family, gradually, but forever.

They were the hardest words I have ever spoken.

"Where will you go?" my father asked me.

"To Mexico, *papà*."

"What will you live on?" he asked.

"I don't know. I'll think of something."

There is a place on the Eiffel Tower that shows the direction and the distance to every country on earth. My mother put her arm around mine and led me to the display, and asked:

"Show me where Mexico is."

I pointed in the general direction, and she bent over the plaque to read the distance. Then she turned to me and said:

"We'll never see you again."

"Sure we'll see each other, *mamma*; maybe less often, but we'll never stop seeing one another," I lied.

In the few days that remained to us, time went galloping past. The hours flew by too fast for us to say everything we were feeling. My efforts to leaven the sadness were awkward, and only sharpened the sense of bewilderment that was slowly taking hold of us all.

The train for Italy left the station at eight in the evening. I couldn't go to see them off. We had already been silent for a while, waiting for the moment when we would have to say goodbye. I burst into tears. My father stepped close to me, took my hands in his, and started crying too.

"Massimo, I don't know what more I can do to help you," he said.

"You've always done your best, *papà*; this is just how it went."

He kept on crying, gripping both my hands in his. My mother was sitting down, staring at the wall. I called to her. She turned to look at me, her face streaked with tears, and she came over to my father and me, wrapping her arms around us both. I walked them to the door. My mother went out first, stroking my hair the way she did when I was a little boy. My *papà* couldn't seem to let go of my hands, he continued to look at them and weep.

"My poor boy, I don't know what else I can do to help you."

"Goodbye, *papà*."

He kissed me on the forehead and caught up with my mother, who was already going down the stairs.

Twenty days later, in a port in Galicia, I boarded a ship bound for Veracruz.

We will glow like lanterns
bright fireflies in July night skies
and we'll live on silk and pearls
pale Ulysses on eclipsed seas

The decision to go to Mexico, as I mentioned before, was fairly haphazard: a book, Alessandra's baseless enthusiasm, and a vague notion of its history and traditions, derived entirely from movies I had seen. I had seen all of the classics: from Eisenstein's *¡Que viva Mexico!* to Peckinpah's *The Wild Bunch*, from Sergio Leone's *A Fistful of Dynamite* to Marlon Brando in *The Appaloosa*. I also knew that Mexico had offered refuge to Trotsky, Vittorio Vidali, and Tina Modotti. In short, compared with the dictatorships and the horrors of the other countries in Central America, it seemed like the least of the possible evils.

The love and the allegiance that I felt toward Cuba and Nicaragua had obliged me to rule them out in my planning from the very first, because I was afraid that I might damage their image if I were arrested there by the Italian police. In reality, for an accidental fugitive, without well-placed government supporters or the money to pay for them, the world is pretty much all the same. If I hadn't stumbled into the lawyer Melvin's trap, I would have been arrested pretty soon anyway, because I was circulating in the most pathetically wrong circles imaginable for a fugitive. I might, perhaps, have managed to stay at liberty for a little longer if I had holed up in some pleasant tourist resort and devoted myself to studying the Maya, Aztec, and Olmec civilizations. But even though I traveled extensively throughout Mexico, exploring the country, I could never manage to break away from Mexico City.

Which is not really Mexico (and I even wonder if it's actually part of the planet Earth); more like an episode from *The Twilight Zone*, where everything conceivable happens, amidst the most complete indifference. This lunatic megalopolis dealt such a violent blow to my awareness and my imagination that I fell completely under the spell of its everyday madness. I lived in a permanent state of bewilderment, tension, and fear.

In the end, with Calle de Soto, Mexico City tore me to shreds.

It's been nine years since I left Mexico, but only since my pardon, and the end of my troubles with the law, have I found myself able to think back to that period. Before, I never had the strength. Now I understand that the "peculiar" quality of my experiences in Mexico derived from the impact and intertwining of two distinct situations, each of them dominated by perverse mechanisms: my personal condition of accidental fugitive and the milieu of the Mexican left, which accepted me and offered me safe haven. When I arrived there, I was exhausted from years of trials, imprisonment, and life on the run, with a special predisposition for catastrophes. In spite of all that, I was pretty certain that my new friends were no better off than I was. The Mexican left had been decimated by reaction and repression, and perennially divided by the ferocious hatred between Trotskyites and Stalinists; by the eighties, it was floundering in a general state of crisis that rendered it flabby, shallow, and inconsistent.

In contrast with European society, where the decline and crisis of the left coincided with a period of social peace and tranquility, Mexico City was a battleground, riven by continuous duels, guerrilla skirmishes, and outright warfare in every walk of life. And this tattered, confused fragment of the left was obliged, by a militant sense of duty, to launch into the battles, in support of this or that struggle. Selflessness and generosity of spirit were never enough; every lunge forward ended in total defeat. There seemed to be a sort of ancillary curse that befell this left-wing milieu; the nature of the curse was that each defeat on the political plane was accompanied by a matching tragedy in the private lives of the militants.

I first came into contact with them at the university. I had enrolled in the history department, and I was especially interested in attending courses on the Mexican revolution. A sociology professor happened to notice me, and began inviting me to parties and dinners where the conversation was always about politics. This sector of the left seemed to spend a lot of time socializing, frequenting salons and chattering endlessly, divided by old resentments that always emerged at the end of the evening, at first with veiled and then increasingly open barbs, and in the end with all-out verbal brawls, insults riveting in like machine gun fire.

And I was often the cause of these furious disputes. I was new to the milieu, and inevitably someone would ask me if was a Trotskyite or a Stalinist. Because I wanted to remain friends with everybody in the group, I would always find myself walking on eggshells, spinning intricate ideological webs in order to give the most neutral possible response. I told them that I had no clearly formulated position because the Italian left had "culpably" failed to address the issue properly, and that I had been a member of an organization, Lotta Continua, that, still more "culpably," had never even explored it.

At that point, as each faction eagerly explained their own positions, the discussion would grow increasingly ferocious, and I would take advantage of the confusion to edge out of the room. Not only did I care nothing at all about this issue; it struck me as hopelessly outdated and even a bit idiotic.

I couldn't tell anyone that, when I was thirteen, I spent all my spare time frequenting a Marxist-Leninist group of a very strict Stalinist persuasion. Every Saturday afternoon, right after the meeting of my Boy Scout troop, I would go to the office of this group in the Via San Giovanni da Verdara, still dressed in my junior explorer uniform (with short pants), and there I would attend the lessons for cadres. But the real attraction luring me to those tiresome weekly meetings was the attendance of a good number of partisans. After the class was over, they would let me sit on their knees and they would recount old stories of the Italian armed resistance and exile in Eastern Europe where they had fled to avoid being sent to prison after being found guilty and sentenced for episodes in the resistance movement.

In that setting, I had grown up with a highly romanticized opinion of Stalin, whom I imagined as a sort of jolly uncle who had done a great deal on behalf of the proletariat of the world. As I grew older and gained political experience, I came to understand that things were a trifle more complex, but my fondness for my partisan "grandpas" had always prevented me from taking a clear position, preferring to avoid the issue. I had always tried to skirt around the matter.

I instinctively disliked the Mexican Trotskyites, whom I found pedantic and irritating, and who seemed to have no other purpose in life than to settle accounts over the murder of their ideological leader.

The first few times I attended these salons and dinners, I practically jumped out of my chair whenever somebody said that the following week their group was planning to go underground. I thought my friends must be reckless fools to bring me into contact with such dangerous individuals, knowing full well that I was living in hiding myself. But, since I saw the same people again week after week, I soon understood that it was all just a pose.

I met some interesting people as well. The most significant friendship I made was with the son of Victor Serge, Vlady, who was considered the world's leading practitioner of Trot-skyite iconography. And he was first and foremost a great artist; I was already familiar with many of his artworks, having seen them in major Mexican museums. I found his technique very striking.

Once we started seeing one another more frequently, he let me come watch him paint. At the time, he was frescoing the walls and ceiling of a new public library in Mexico City. I would spend days at a time watching him work.

I saw him as a physical link with the national school of Mex-ican art that constituted the only true example in our times of a perfect integration of art and society, and which produced such figures as Orozco, Rivera, Siqueiros, and Kalho. It was a pitiless, brutal, orotund school of art, the creation of artists who always worked in close contact with the people and who revived and gave new dignity to native tradition. Vlady was the last working artist of that generation, and for me, spending time with him meant experiencing directly a piece of history, immortalized by masters of line and color.

He worked with only one assistant, an elderly Indio who mixed his paints for him. I soon realized that the old man was far more than just a helper; he was in fact Vlady's closest advis-er. When he disliked something or was unpersuaded by an approach, the Indio expressed his disappointment by turning irritable and intractable. Vlady himself wasn't the easiest per-son to get along with, and so the two would soon clash, and spectacularly vivid quarrels would ensue. And whenever they fought, Vlady's wife would butt in. She was a former nurse, as disagreeable as could be, and it seemed to me that Vlady would have been delighted to be rid of her.

I remember one time when Vlady had just finished painting an enormous dinosaur skeleton upon which a tiny Fidel Castro was riding, and he was preparing to sketch, on a smaller wall, a portrait of Freud on a square panel of burlap that he had glued to the wall. The old Indio wasn't happy about this experimentation with burlap, and started to bang the floor with the cans of paint he was bringing to the maestro.

Vlady stopped working and they began to argue with all their usual vim. That was when I understood what an important role the Indio assistant played. He might not have known who Freud was, but he had such a well-developed artistic sensibility that he could understand what people—his own people—would see in that square of burlap. He explained his thoughts to the maestro and, as always, Vlady paid heed. It struck me more than once that to Vlady, this elderly Indio represented the eyes of the people for whom he painted and to whom he dedicated his creations.

Vlady was a man who was tormented by his own past. Following his father, he had already experienced, as a child, the pain of exile, Siberia, and the long voyage by ship to Mexico, the only country willing to accept Victor Serge. Ideological disputes that followed the death of Trotsky had separated them, and had obliged Victor to live the last years of his life in an unjust and painful state of isolation. Whenever Vlady spoke of his father, it was clear that he was plagued by a sense of guilt for their separation during the last years of Victor's life.

He had inherited crates full of unpublished writings. One day, he let me and my sociology professor look through the papers. We immediately understood the historic importance of the material. We tried to persuade Vlady to make the papers available to the public, but he refused. A few days later I was arrested, and I never heard anything more about the artist or those documents.

The people I socialized with were not only students and intellectuals, but also labor organizers and factory workers, but I wasn't likely to run into them in the salons. We would run into one another fairly often during the various protests we took part in. I had a heartfelt admiration for them, and it was beyond me why they continued to spend time with the intellectual class, likeable as people but politically deleterious.

They were hungry for news about the European movement and whenever we met, they would eagerly compare our experiences. They were looking for a different organizational approach, one that might allow them to resolve at least one aspect of the general crisis. For my part, I did everything I could to discourage them from seeking that new model in Europe, where every approach adopted—without exception—had proved disastrous.

Women were a tiny minority in the group but whenever it was necessary to appear at a so-called "mass demonstration," the comrades would show up with an entourage of wives and children, and the imbalance became less apparent.

They were always supremely conscious of my status as a fugitive, and whenever things heated up, a couple of guys would make sure I was hustled off to a quieter neighborhood.

My love of photography offered me a way to make myself useful. My photography was actually pretty good and a few of my shots were published in movement magazines.

On one occasion, photography came close to getting me killed. A vast area of one of the *ciudades perdidas*—cluttered with illegal hovels that were home to *campesinos* who had been kicked off the land and converted en masse into homeless beggars—was slated for clearing to make way for an industrial plant being built by one of the usual North American corporations.

In those days (and I doubt it's any different now) it was a well-established practice that the purchase price for land illegally occupied by poor squatters included the armed intervention of the police. The *mordida* (or 'bite,' a Mexican term for bribes and corruption) was something more than an ethical problem. In fact, in Mexico, it constituted a way of life for the police force itself. Right up to the top. The chief of police of

Mexico City, for instance, whom the opposition press accused of controlling a prostitution ring of over twelve thousand *putas*, was arrested in the United States in 1984 and charged with international cocaine trafficking. Moreover, whenever the police were called upon to perform a mass eviction, not only did they expect a lavish bribe to be shared out, but also claimed a right to plunder, looting the evictees of what little they owned.

At the first light of dawn, truckloads of policemen in full riot gear arrived on the scene, followed by the bulldozers that would flatten the shantytown, as well as other empty trucks, which would be loaded with the booty from the planned mass eviction. The activists and the slum-dwellers had been waiting for the police all night long, and were ready for what was coming. Everybody knew that there was really nothing to be done and that, yet again, for the thousandth but certainly not the last time, their rights would be crushed underfoot. But, after a long and exhausting assembly, they had decided to resist.

The fighting went on for hours. I was stationed on a nearby overpass, where I enjoyed an excellent vantage point from which to take pictures with my telephoto lens. As the police progressively seized control of one patch of land after another, the squads of looters would move in, followed by the bulldozers. I stopped taking pictures after the tenth roll of film. I felt nauseous. With the sense of bewilderment that I always felt in the presence of the madness that was Mexico City, with which I had discovered I was fully capable of coexisting, I sat smoking a cigarette and watching the mayhem.

And that's how a passing patrol car found me when it pulled to a stop, its occupants suspicious at the sight of my camera. I hadn't noticed them before they screeched to a halt, and my reaction of startled fear gave them an additional cause for suspicion. They understood that I wasn't just a chance passerby, so they wanted to take me in for questioning and further checking. For an instant, the end seemed near, and then my survival instincts sprang into action. With a calm voice and a string of smiles, I started bargaining for my freedom.

The police drove off with my camera, my money, my jacket, and my Timberlands. I sat back down. And smoked. And watched.

Alessandra brought me another camera from Europe. Taking advantage of the fact that various friends came to Mexico, I had put together a small import business selling photographic equipment, which commanded impossibly high prices in Mexico. I also imported a special kind of drawing paper, very popular with artists and almost impossible to find there. This allowed me to round out my modest earnings as a translator. All things considered, as cheap as it was to live there, I was doing reasonably well. In any case, in Mexico as well, the burden of expense was borne by my family.

Word got out that I was running an interesting import-export business, and I received orders for everything you could think of. One guy even asked me to get him a Vespa. The Mexican government's trade barriers prohibited the importation of motorcycles, and the local production, monopolized by a single company, was insufficient for the demand among the young people who could afford them. Many young people managed to smuggle them in from the United States, but then they couldn't ride them openly, because the police would surely confiscate them. A few motorcycle aficionados had organized a protest movement. They staged demonstrations every Sunday, with a thundering illegal procession of bikes rolling down Insurgentes, the broad north-south boulevard that runs through the center of the city. It was a funny sight: a cluster of festive, rumbling motorbikes zipping by, chased by another cluster of cops, also on motorbikes. It was like an old Keystone Kops routine.

Sunday was a strange day in Mexico City. An unnatural sense of calm extended over the whole city, as if it was catching its breath after an exhausting week.

Everything was closed in my neighborhood, and I took advantage of that to leave the house early and take a leisurely stroll down to Calle Benjamin Hill, where Victor Serge had lived just before his death. I would stand looking at his apartment building; deep down, I was invoking the spirit of the great revolutionary and asking him to impart an inspiration that might change my life. Or at least give me a good excuse to leave that city once and for all.

Then I would head lazily back home, stopping on the way to buy a couple of pieces of corn from a street vendor who lived in an old, foul-smelling shack. He boiled the corn up juicy and delicious. I think he considered me his most amusing customer. After a lengthy and laborious period of familiarization, I managed to explain how I liked my corn. He fixed me two pieces. I liked them boiling hot, spread with butter and mayonnaise, and then sprinkled with a copious layer of powdered spicy red chili pepper. I would eat everything with lots of chili powder. It was the only reliable remedy for diarrhea, or Montezuma's revenge, as the gringos called it. Anything that had been in contact with water caused intestinal problems; at first, I stuffed myself with pharmaceutical remedies but after a while I took the advice of my local friends and used chili pepper, the only effective natural remedy.

On every faucet in the house, I had installed very expensive filters, but they didn't do much good. I drank Pepsi and beer, and to wash fruit and vegetables I used Tehuacán mineral water, the only brand produced by the state. I bought huge jerricans of the water at the American supermarket in my neighborhood.

Another obligatory stop along my route was "El Farolito," a legendary little taco stand, specializing in *tortas*, or grilled sandwiches. There I would complete my Sunday brunch, with a decisive shift toward the savory—two *tortas* with steak, avocado, and hot sauce, washed down with a couple of beers—in a complete reversal of my weekday routine, owing to the simple fact that the pastry shop run by German immigrants, where I usually had breakfast, was closed on Sundays.

Around noon, I would head back home and make a round of phone calls to see if anyone had anything interesting planned for the day. Usually I would leave the house, not to return until late that evening. If nobody had any plans, I would phone over to Brema, a restaurant that is renowned for its Mitteleuropean menu, to reserve a table.

For a certain period I spent my Sundays in the countryside near Cuernavaca, where a friend had persuaded me to go into business with him as part owner of a flock of sheep. We were raising them to be slaughtered for meat. We had rented a fenced field, and we hired a shepherd to keep an eye on them. Every week we drove out to take a look at our future earnings, busily grazing and fattening themselves up.

The shepherd was a likable guy; his wife, a homely chatterbox, was said to be a bit of a *bruja* (sorceress). In conversation, she had admitted that this was true, but that she merely knew the properties and uses of local herbs. After lunch, she took us on a little tour over the fields, pointing out various plants and explaining their beneficial effects. That stroll was the only part of the day I enjoyed. To spend a Sunday watching sheep—even if those sheep were half mine—didn't strike me as a very smart use of my day. The least appealing part of the day, though, was definitely lunch. Our shepherd had decided that the finest specialty of the area was armadillo, and there wasn't a single Sunday that his wife failed to cook us up an armadillo—but only after clubbing the critter to death before our eyes.

As usual, the whole thing was triggered by a misunderstanding, caused by my own excessive courtesy as a guest. The first time they served armadillo, despite the fact it tasted foul, I had said, "How delightful!" Those two words sealed my fate for many Sundays to come. Each time we drove out into the countryside, I would solemnly resolve to point out that maybe it was time to change the bill of fare, but the woman showered us with such a hail of conversation that I never managed to get out the words. Part of the problem was that my friend really liked armadillo. "It tastes sort of like *cerdolito* (suckling pig)," he would say, "but a little gamier. It has all the flavors of the countryside." Just then, I was beginning to hate him.

Once, when I found an especially greasy piece of meat on my plate, a strange association of ideas prompted me to pour a little Coca-Cola over it. Strangely enough, this actually improved the flavor. It no longer tasted unholy and foul. It was merely disgusting.

There are times when I think that if someone were to ask me to name the five worst things I had done in my life, one might be "having eaten armadillo repeatedly." In any case, one fine day I decided I couldn't take it anymore. I sold my share of the flock.

One member of the group, a union officer at the telephone company, had inherited a house and some land on the volcanic hills surrounding Mexico City. We would go out there frequently to have barbecues and play soccer; between games and meals, we would talk, as usual, about politics. Every so often, I would shut out the conversation and gaze down at the megalopolis stretching out beneath us for miles and miles in every direction.

"I don't like you, I don't like you one little bit!" I would think to myself.

At certain times of the day, a giant cowl of pale-red gas loured over the city; that was our daily dose of pollution. Even ten years ago, ecologists had sounded alarm bells, warning that

Mexico City was a region at extreme environmental risk. Recently I read that the pollution there caused thirty thousand deaths a year. It is believed that another four million people suffer from pollution-caused diseases. The administration of the Federal District, then as now, comes up with solutions straight out of science fiction. One such solution was to build huge fans on the surrounding mountains, to force a mass of clean air down into the city and sweep away the toxic cloud.

The group had no idea of how to organize a political movement around environmental issues. In fact, pollution seemed like the least of the city's problems compared with the challenges that the populace faced in simply making it through each day with a shred of dignity still intact. We all knew, for instance, that the uncontrolled development of the city had created huge clusters of population around dangerous and toxic factories and plants, but to raise that issue would mean provoking the anger of the local inhabitants and the factory workers themselves.

We were talking about that very subject, sitting on the grass in front of the house, when the Pemex (Petróleos Mexicanos) plant blew up. There was a roar, a burst of flame, and then a cloud of smoke, dense and black as pitch, billowed up over part of the city. We immediately got in our cars and started down to the city, but it was impossible to get close to the disaster area. Wild rumors were circulating about the number of dead; radio and television news reports received their marching orders from the government, who tried to minimize the scale of the disaster.

Without success. By the following day, the opposition press had already reported the truth. The blast had destroyed not only the oil facility itself, but the entire slum area that surrounded it. And as if that weren't enough, subsequent to the initial explosion, underground fuel lines exploded, demolishing rows of homes in outlying neighborhoods. It was impossible to arrive at a specific number of deaths because the government had immediately ordered a number of mass graves dug, with the justification that, otherwise, contagious diseases might spread. The official government numbers—about two thousand victims—were based exclusively on a count of the corpses that had been identified by relatives or bodies found with identification papers.

This report triggered a wave of furious indignation because it was well known that most of the inhabitants of the shanty towns were Salvadoran and Guatemalan refugees, or else Indios from Chiapas and other poor sections of Mexico, and therefore *indocumentados*, or undocumented. The survivors were abandoned to shift for themselves, in an intolerable state of deprivation. On the fifth day, when we finally succeeded in making our way through the army and police cordon surrounding the site, we found people in a state of frenzied desperation.

It wasn't difficult to persuade the survivors to appoint a committee to demand government aid and reparations from Pemex. It was clear that the company was seriously at fault; it had used antiquated facilities, placing demands upon the plant that far exceeded its capacity. That, plus the total absence of safety regulations, caused the explosion. A huge protest movement immediately began to spread, and when it really began to irritate those in power, government and industry decided that it was time to put an end to the discussion once and for all.

The representatives of the communities that had been devastated by the blast were either bought off or frightened into silence. My friends did all they could to keep the committee alive, until the comrade from our group who had been most vocal and visible in public meetings was killed by a hit-and-run driver.

That's when we withdrew from the struggle, and went back

to playing soccer in the meadow at the mountain house, talking about politics and looking down at the city below us.

During an unsuccessful attempt to organize a strike among
the factory workers at a Japanese auto plant to protest the dangerous conditions there (the workers on the spray-painting line
were not even given respirator masks), I met Odile.

Odile was French. She wrote and illustrated children's books.
She was married to a Mexican labor organizer she had met in
Paris. They had two children, a four-year-old boy and a two-
year-old girl. Odile was a sweet-tempered, energetic woman. It
was not easy for her to live in Mexico City, in a low-income
neighborhood that was steadily collapsing under the weight of
the uncontrolled urban development—it was estimated that
three thousand new homes were being built every day. Still, she
managed to make everything she did look easy and natural.
She conveyed a sense of peace and confidence. I liked to spend
time with her; often, we sat in silence. I was happy just to sit
and watch her draw the fanciful characters that populated her
children's stories.

One morning, Bulmaro, her husband, called me on the
phone:

"Odile lost our son," he told me.

"I'm sorry to hear that; did she have an abortion? I didn't
know she was pregnant," I replied.

"No, I'm talking about Julio. She lost him on the subway."

"How the hell can you lose a child on the subway?" I
protested.

"Get over here, we need your help," he cut me off, hanging
up without saying goodbye.

The others were already at their house when I got there. As
I looked around at their somber, worried faces, I immediately
understood that this was serious.

It had all happened in seconds. Odile had walked down into

the subway station during rush hour, holding the little girl in her arms, the boy by the hand. They had immediately been swallowed up by the usual overwhelming throng of passengers. Odile tried to make her way onto a subway car, pushing the boy ahead of her. As soon as he stepped into the car, the crowd lurched and swayed, forcing her to let go of his hand. In that fraction of a second, the doors closed. The train pulled out of the station.

I had been in the Mexico City subway system just once. After that I stuck to the public bus system and occasionally used *peseros*, the collective taxis. That one time, I was literally forced to fight my way onto the train and off again, and I had my pocket picked to boot. It wasn't something I wanted to experience again, and I imagined that only a fourth-generation native of Mexico City would be up to the ordeal. I would never have dreamed that Odile would use the subway, much less take the children with her.

The child's disappearance had already been reported to the police and the subway authorities. Deep down, I thought that was enough; it seemed like the others, who were already organizing a full-blown search campaign, were a little over the top. We split up into teams, and each team went to a station along the train line. Bulmaro stayed at home to coordinate the operation by phone. They even reached out to a number of former *panchitos*, who were now supporters of the group, to see what they could achieve through their contacts with the criminals that infested the subway system.

Odile was nowhere to be seen. Shut in her room with her baby daughter, she was in a state of shock.

There were about ten of us in each search team. My team was assigned to the station after the one where Odile had lost the boy. We talked to hundreds of people, until the subway closed down for the night; we offered rewards. Once an hour we phoned Bulmaro, but the answer was always the same: *nada*.

I realized I had underestimated the gravity of the situation when, as I made my way around the station, I began noticing little posters with lots of different photographs. Photographs of children. In Mexico City, children went missing all the time. On the subway, in the street, from their homes—they weren't always found.

On the third day, we wallpapered the stations with photographs of little Julio. On the tenth day we stopped searching.

Spending ten days in a subway station searching for a four-year-old boy was an experience that will stay with me for the rest of my life. Not merely because of the desperation that gripped me every minute of those ten days, but especially because of my sense of helplessness in the face of a city so huge that it could swallow up anything, anyone, without explanation, as if they had never existed. Amidst the most absolute indifference. Even a little boy that you had seen playing until just a few hours ago.

My presence as a gringo in the subway station hardly went unobserved. I was the chosen target of profiteers, interested only in scamming a little money out of the situation. They would come up to me, acting as if they knew something, and only after I had slipped them a bank note or two would they try to palm off fanciful tales that only wasted our time.

By the time it was over, it was obvious that someone had kidnapped the boy. But who? And why? None of us really wanted to know, but the former *panchitos* put us in touch with child-traffickers (illegal adoptions, the organ trade, and snuff films). They took lots of money from us and never told us anything useful.

I saw places I had never even heard of, like the dormitories for abandoned children. Where, for a peso, they spent the night and felt a little safer. A haven till the next day, when they ventured back out into the streets, to beg, to shine shoes, or to steal. Streets where mothers prostituted their eight-, nine-, and ten-year-old daughters, for a handful of coins.

For the authorities, Julio's disappearance was just one more file to put with the countless others that already filled their filing cabinets to overflowing. For Odile and Bulmaro, it marked the end of everything. After a few months, she went back to France with her little girl. He stayed in Mexico, but he was never the same.

Political activism remained his only interest; he seemed to be unstoppable, tireless, but he scrupulously avoided any situation where there was the slightest risk of human contact. He was no longer seen at parties or dinners. The comrades told me that sooner or later he would get over it and become the same old Bulmaro. They all agreed that he had been right to stay in Mexico instead of following Odile back to France. He needed to stay with his people, they said, he shouldn't leave the group. He shouldn't abandon the cause.

I saw things differently. I was a friend of Bulmaro's and one evening, when all the others were at a birthday party, I went to his house and knocked on the door.

"Hi, Bulmaro, I've come to have a talk with you."

"It must be a long talk if you brought a bottle of liquor."

"Yes, that's right," I answered, showing him the label. "This is calvados from Normandy, aged twelve years. I brought it with me from France, and I was saving it for an important occasion."

"Then this must be an important talk you have in mind. I've never tasted this liquor, what's it like?"

"It's brandy made out of apple cider. Normandy is a beautiful place, Bulmaro, a proud, fierce land, windswept. This calvados will give you a whiff of the place."

"Max, I'm happy you've come to see me, but if you want to talk about Odile, France, and my children, then you can just take your bottle back home with you."

"No, Bulmaro, I'm not leaving. Even if we have to duke it out, you're still going to listen to what I have to say to you."

"You're too big for me, Italian comrade . . . Come on in, I guess this means you're going to spoil my evening."

We sat down, facing one another, across a little square table where I had seen the children eating dinner many times before. Between us stood the bottle, two glasses, an ashtray, and our cigarettes.

"Bulmaro, why won't you go to Paris to be with Odile?"

"Because I'm Mexican, Max. Because I am a Mexican labor organizer, and my place is here, in Mexico. If I went to France, I would be throwing away the most important thing in my life up till now."

"Horseshit, Bulmaro, that's horseshit. If you said you were staying here because you still hoped that you could find your son, I'd understand. But that would be horseshit, too, because you know perfectly well"—I hesitated for an instant—"that you'll never find him. But don't tell me you're staying here for the cause, because I don't believe it for a second."

He shot to his feet and grabbed the back of his chair with both hands, squeezing it powerfully.

"You're laying it down a little heavy tonight, Italian comrade. Why don't you go back to Italy? You come here, you swagger around, you call me a liar. Everyone who has known me all my life says I am doing the right thing. You're just a Johnny-come-lately, you have no right to tell me what to do."

"Bulmaro"—and my voice expressed my sympathy and understanding—"all the others are just afraid of losing you. Can't you see? There's only a few of you left, and if you left the group might fall apart, because everyone sees their failure to find the *niño* as the worst sort of defeat. This city has screwed you once again, and nobody wants to admit it. If you chose your family instead of the group, you would throw the group into total disarray."

"That's not true." He shoved the chair to one side and sat down again, his shoulders slumping. "If there were any social justice in this country, children wouldn't disappear. The group has drawn new strength from this tragedy. We will continue the struggle. It is Odile who was wrong to leave. She surrendered, and took my daughter away from me. As a mother, she should have stayed, in the hope of finding the boy."

Something inside me began to rebel. I didn't want to listen to him anymore.

"Odile did the right thing by leaving. Julio's not coming back, Bulmaro. He's dead. Get it into your head: Julio is dead!"

I'd said it. Till then, no one had dared to say what everyone knew for certain. To scream it right into Bulmaro's face had been a catharsis, perhaps even for him.

"Listen," I continued. "Odile went to Paris to save her own life and the girl's life. She couldn't stay here to wallow in grief and guilt. It was her duty as a mother, Bulmaro, her duty to keep on living. You need to go be with her. You might be able to start over, maybe have another child, replace death with life. This is your family. Otherwise, you'll be alone for the rest of your life, alone with your regrets. Hanging on to politics is an excuse, a wall you're hiding behind so that you don't have to look at reality. Mexico will follow its destiny, with you or without you. You're not a leader, Bulmaro. You're a good labor organizer, you're a staunch Communist and you'd give your life for the cause, but the cause doesn't need your life. Your family needs it. I said what I needed to say, and now I can leave. But believe me, I came here tonight only because I love you."

He put his hand on my arm. "Don't go, Max. Please. I don't want to be alone again tonight."

We sat, not looking at one another, lost in our respective thoughts, drinking and smoking in silence. I didn't know what else to say. Suddenly, in a desperate attempt to regain the sense of closeness that had vanished, I asked him:

"What are you thinking about?"

Bulmaro looked up.

"Odile. I can't go to Paris, Max. I couldn't look her in the eye, because I can't stop thinking that it's her fault Julio is gone. I hate her for that."

For the second time, I felt a profound sense of rejection. I loved Odile, and I knew how much she already hated herself for what had happened. I stubbed out my cigarette and replied:

"That's wrong to say, Bulmaro. It wasn't her fault. Certainly, if that's how you feel about it, you'd better stay away from her. Odile is a special woman, and I hope that you don't regret losing her one day. Sometimes life is truly indecent. You have a chance at a great love story, and you're flushing it down the toilet. I'm sorry, but I don't understand you. I'm in a completely different situation. There's a woman that I've loved since I was fifteen, I want to live with her, and I can't. Actually, if she left me it would be better for both of us."

"Max, why are you saying these things?"

"Because I am a man who has borrowed his freedom. Tonight, tomorrow, in ten years, they'll catch up with me. It would be wrong, it would be senseless to drag her down in the wreckage of my life."

"Why don't you leave her? I think that's your decision, Max. Find the courage to leave her."

"I've tried, but love is strange, Bulmaro. It hides reality from you and it makes you clutch at the most forlorn hopes. I've told her how I feel, but deep down I know I could never say good-bye to her. I feel like an emotional vampire, sucking love out of everyone I meet. And especially from her. You know what the best solution would be for me, Bulmaro? To die, without anyone knowing, to disappear into the void, like your little boy. I would cause some grief for those who love me, but a grief full of questions, which is one step down from absolute grief. It would let everybody have a chance to go back to their lives, a chance that you, my friend, are throwing out the window. And above all, I would win my battle, because then they'd never catch me, and not knowing that I was dead, they would continue to consider me a fugitive, a wanted man, for all time."

"You're drunk, Max."

"Sure I am, Bulmaro. But I know what I'm talking about."

I looked at him. He seemed surprised.

"I've never heard you talk about yourself. The comrades and I just thought you were a cold guy, like the snow on your Alps. But you're just hopeless."

Yes, we were friends again. With a smile, I answered him: "Good old Mexican comrades, you've fumbled the critical analysis once again!" Bulmaro let me fill his glass of calvados once more. He took another sip and said:

"Listen, Max, explain to me why you came here. This place isn't safe for you."

"Bulmaro, I'm not sure exactly why I came here. In my situation, one place is as good as another. I don't like Mexico, it scares me, and it's only hurt me so far. But what scares me even more is the idea of changing again, of starting over somewhere else. The only thing I care about is staving off the inevitable, every day that I remain free means that I can defend my innocence a little more powerfully, give a meaning to this battle I've been fighting since 1976."

"What you're saying is crazy."

"No, Bulmaro, what they did to me is crazy."

"What meaning is there to this kind of life?"

"None. It's just the price I pay to annoy my judges."

"Now you're the one talking horseshit, Max. Forget about your judges and start living again. There must be a place somewhere on this earth where you can start a new life."

"I don't want a new life, Bulmaro. I want the life I used to have."

After that evening, I thought frequently about my conversation with Bulmaro. Talking like this had reawakened in me all those conflicts that I had instead worked so hard, for such a long time, to lull to sleep. I tried to understand this state of mind, explaining it away with the fact that I was "too European," and therefore it was impossible for me to accept what had happened to Julio, Odile, and Bulmaro without some rational explanation. And so, for a long time, I decided not to see anyone from the group.

My friends in exile back in Paris were right: I was too delicate for the third world. My mental and physical state was steadily deteriorating. I was successfully keeping my panic attacks under control but, unlike before, I was going through long periods of abulia. During those spells, I experienced the present solely in terms of regret. I had lost all hope of seeking a new life because I felt the future was imprisoned by my awkward past. In the end the guilty verdict, so unjust and so disgraceful, had become something I could not overcome.

In order to escape from this situation of hopelessness, I found myself daydreaming about unlikely surprise twists in the appeals process and my ensuing triumphal return home. When I snapped out of these vivid fantasies and looked around, what I saw was truly depressing. That was when I began to consider the possibility of waging a new legal battle to reopen my case. The idea wasn't mine. One of my lawyers had come up with it. He still hadn't given up on the idea of obtaining justice, and he had submitted a motion with the court to preserve the trial evidence, indispensable for reopening the case. I knew that the odds were against me. The Rocco code (enacted under Mussolini and still in effect) allowed for new trials in only an exceedingly narrow range of instances.

I didn't know what to do with my life. I could go back to Italy and wait for my lawyers to submit a motion for a new trial to the Court of Cassation. But it seemed to me unfair that I should spend more time in jail, and so I decided to leave Mexico only if my case was resolved in my favor. Other times, I thought it would be best to forget about my past life and try to obtain Mexican citizenship. And when I was overwhelmed by despair, I gave up on finding any solution at all, and sank into my morass of abulia, waiting for fate to work its will.

In that sense, my encounter with Melvin Cervera Sanchez gave a fairly random turn to my life, because it came about just when I was opting in favor of Mexican citizenship and not for a return to Italy.

During the time when I was avoiding the group, I took refuge at the university and began to hang out, in my free time, with foreign students, most of them from the US and Japan. Mexico City was a world that didn't concern them, and they even managed to consider it picturesque. They saw the city as tourists, even when they spent four or five years there. In that way, they managed to see only the things they liked. The worst thing that could happen to them was to be shaken down for a little money by the police.

I was especially well liked by the Japanese, who invited me to all their parties. There, they inevitably cajoled me into making them some Italian or French food and to dance. I didn't particularly enjoy dancing because my size made it hard to move with any agility; vigorous activity would make sweat pour off me. But once, in an attempt to offer a courteous refusal to their invitations, I told them the only dance I knew was the twist, certain that no one could possibly remember it, and that the records were impossible to find. But nothing is impossible for the Japanese, and at the next party I found they had managed to collect a substantial portion of the world production of twist recordings, and even more astonishing, they had learned to dance the twist.

Often, on Saturday afternoons, they would take me with them to watch Mexican wrestling, where they constituted a special cheering section. I thought the Japanese were a lot of fun, and perhaps a bit childish—with their enthusiasm for everything they did, work and play, and their absolute lack of any historical depth. I met Japanese people who had never heard of Hitler and who had only the vaguest idea of their national history. Obviously, I was hanging out with science students, not students from the history department. On evenings when we had nothing in particular to do, they would ask me to tell them stories. I would talk to them about the Renaissance, the Enlightenment, or the French Revolution as if they were fairy tales by Hans Christian Andersen.

The young women were almost all married to computer experts who had found a genuine gold mine in the backward expanses of Mexico. The bachelors were for the most part students attracted by the low cost of studying at the university and the desire to marry a Mexican girl, as they never tired of saying. It was the fashionable thing.

Kioko was twenty years old. She had gotten married in a hurry to a brainy, boring older guy; but she fell in love with me and began to court me relentlessly.

I met her at the university. She was attending a Spanish course for foreigners, where I would go with other university students to browse, as it were, in search of new female students to befriend, and to watch as the Japanese students took their orals, which we found hilarious. The course was not limited to language; it also taught a smattering of Mexican customs. One piece of protocol that was taught was the Mexican way of shaking hands, a four-part ceremony: a straightforward handshake, a back-of-the-hand variant, straight again, and then a jovial slap on the right shoulder with the left hand. For the Japanese, generally unaccustomed to physical contact with other human beings, this was a challenging routine, and there was a fair bit of irresistible slapstick when the professor would break the class up into couples to practice this form of greeting. In particular, they found it impossible to eliminate the traditional bow. Thus, they would take one step backward, make a little bow, step forward, perform a Mexican-style handshake and, after a resounding slap on the shoulder, step back again for a final bow. They thought it was as funny as we did, and they would laugh till they wept. And it was between one Mexican handshake and another that she and I locked gazes, and stared into one another's eyes till the end of the lesson.

Kioko wasn't very good at languages, and it was several weeks before we were able to speak our first few words. In the meantime, we played at exchanging glances and subtle hints. At first, I wasn't particularly interested in getting involved with her. I had other concerns at the time. But I didn't mind being courted; it had been quite a while since that had happened to me, and it was a nice distraction from my constant state of mental pressure.

She invited me to a party at her house to celebrate the arrival of her brother, who was vacationing in Mexico City for a couple of weeks. He was a comedian on Japanese TV, and we had to spend the entire evening watching videos of his latest shows. I met her husband, too, a short, peevish, balding forty-year-old. He seemed to have sensed what was going on, because he avoided me the whole time I was at his house.

I saw her again a few days later. I was waiting for a bus and noticed that Kioko's Nissan was parked about a hundred feet from the bus stop. She was with a girlfriend, and both of them pretended that they were there by chance. The suspicion dawned on me that they were planning to follow the bus to see where I lived; I knew that all the Japanese students were curious about that because I was the only one who never invited the others over, and whenever anyone asked me where I lived I always gave vague replies. And in fact, the car pulled in behind the bus and never shook the tail once during the forty-minute ride. That day, I walked into a department store that had a rear entrance and lost them. But Kioko was pretty stubborn. In the end I let her follow me home to keep from arousing her suspicions. She parked her car outside the front gate and walked in as if it were the most natural thing imaginable.

Our relationship lasted until I was arrested. The only thing that kept it going was her desire to be with me; I would never contact her myself, and in public we kept our distance. Whenever she felt like it, she would come by my house, and if I was there she came in. Otherwise she'd leave a note.

I never understood what she liked about me. I couldn't always fully maintain my cover as a student/tourist. Sometimes she'd see me in the throes of one of my anxiety attacks, and she would massage my back, hoping that would cure it. She was too young and too Japanese to understand my political beliefs and the sea of troubles in which I was thrashing and floundering. My bedroom was wallpapered with posters of revolutionary political leaders. When she asked who they were, singling out a poster of Lenin, and then seemed satisfied when I answered that he was "an Italian actor from the silent movie era," I realized that I had nothing to fear from her.

I don't know if she loved me; she certainly found me amusing, and laughed at the stories I told her. She told me that her husband was boring, and that she couldn't wait to come see me so that we could make love and then stretch out and she could listen to my voice for hours. I was fond of her. She was sweet and gentle, and most important of all, she was the only carefree person I met in all those years.

For a while, there was a hybrid social group of Americans and Japanese, with the addition of one Italian (me), an Irishman, and a Brazilian woman. We mostly organized excursions and parties. The Yankees were all white Reagan supporters, and the only way to tolerate them was to scatter them around, diluting them among the groups of various nationalities. One of the Yankees—Bob—got Cassandra, the Brazilian woman, pregnant. For some mysterious reason, she decided to turn to me for help and advice. I was the least suitable person imaginable, and I wasn't especially flattered to have been singled out. All the same, after she asked repeatedly, I agreed to go have a talk with Bob, the careless American. He made it blindingly clear to me that the matter was none of his concern.

I still wasn't ready to get back in touch with my friends who had good connections with the medical world, so I advised Cassandra to go see the gynecologist at the university health center. I went with her. The doctor thought that I was Bob, and gave me a long and excruciating lecture on love, sex, and children. I made no effort to set him straight; the situation was already sufficiently painful for Cassandra, and it did no good to make matters even more complicated. All the same, the gynecologist was a reasonably understanding person. He arranged for Cassandra to have a quick abortion in a private clinic. Cassandra was very wealthy, the daughter of a prominent livestock breeder, but I still had to lend her the money for the abortion. She paid me back a little at a time, to avoid having to explain things to her father.

When I got tired of the endless idle banter of my student friends, I tried to find opportunities to go see the rest of the country. While attending a course on the military history of Zapata's cavalry, I learned that they were looking for six volunteers to go interview the last surviving veterans.

Of the six, I was the only non-Mexican. We drove down in an old, beat-up Volkswagen microbus to Cuernavaca, Puebla, Guadalajara, Zacatecas, Morelia, and Jalapa. We visited museums and libraries, we contacted historians and journalists, and, much further south, in Chiapas, we managed to track down three veterans of Zapata's cavalry who were sufficiently alert to be interviewed.

They were poor *campesinos*, and at first they were obse-quious and uncomfortable in front of the video camera and the tape recorder. When they finally felt at their ease, they began to show their old pride at having belonged to the elite division of a revolutionary army.

I already knew from the movies that it had been a harsh war. But I was astonished to learn that they took no prisoners because they had no way to feed them, and that they were forced to abandon their wounded, because they had neither medicine nor doctors to care for them.

Their accounts were very detailed, and it emerged quite clearly that Zapata's troops were considerably more ideological than Villa's. The land, the agrarian reform, and the *revolución incumplida* were deeply rooted concepts in each of these three veterans.

I could not help but consider as naïve and infinitely roman-tic their certainty that Emiliano Zapata had never died, and that he still rode by night through the mountains. They were certain that one day he would ride down to complete the rev-olution and implement agrarian land reform. They were still ready to follow him. In order to persuade us they were serious, they dug up old rusty Mauser muskets, and showed them off proudly.

When I returned to the university, I wrote my report and went on at some length about the myth of Zapata and how it undermined the *campesinos*' ability to construct a real path toward social emancipation. I wished I could believe the same things as the three veterans. In my bedroom, between the posters of Che and Sandino, a poster of their general had pride of place. I considered Zapata to be the finest figure of that unfortunate revolution. I believed, however, that the Mexican proletariat needed to make a break with the past and seek a new path. And I believed that the factory workers of the cen-ter and north would point the way.

The south, according to my analysis, had no place in the struggle. When I visited the south, I was impressed by its natural beauty and by the widespread racism against the Indios. In particular, I had been impressed by the fact that Mexico's southern border divided ethnic groups, all of Maya origin, who spoke the same language, practiced the same customs, and had the same historical memories. For them, that whole region was like a single large house, but to go from one room to another they needed a passport.

I had taken one of these trips to help two friends bring home one of their cousins, who had been thrown in jail for trashing a church. He had taken a trip to Chiapas, purchased a shopping bag full of *mota* (marijuana), and smoked practically the whole thing in the only cool, quiet place he could find—the local church. He had then mistaken the place for an amusement park.

We went to see the parish priest. Like most of the priests in Central America, he worked on behalf of the poor and to defend the Indios. He said that he was sorry our friend had got into trouble; he assured us that he hadn't called the police; it had been the noise from the church that attracted their attention. We gave him money to cover the damage, and we told him how sorry we were about what had happened. Then we went to see the only lawyer-*qua*-coyote in town. In exchange for a truly reasonable fee, he got our friend out of jail. We went to meet him at the gate of the Cerro Hueco prison, and we took him to the church to make his apologies to the priest.

I had heard about Cerro Hueco. I had heard the story of an Indio who fell victim to one of the most absurd miscarriages of justice in history. The Indio was charged with murdering his father, and sentenced to thirty years in prison. Apparently he had confessed to the murder and signed the transcript of his confession with an X mark. During the trial, he appeared relaxed and meek, and he'd listened to the reading of the verdict and sentence without batting an eye.

An old man would come to the prison every day to bring him food. The old man wasn't always allowed to see the Indio, because that was entirely subject to the whims of the guards. Otherwise, they ignored the inmate and his relative. After all, they were just Indios; why worry about them?

One day, a Mexican parliamentarian, a member of the opposition party, went to visit the prison, and a number of the inmates told him that the Indio, of Tzotzil Maya descent, spoke no Spanish, and moreover had no idea of why he had been thrown into prison. The member of parliament investigated briefly, and discovered that the old visitor was none other than the Indio's father, officially the murder victim. Obviously unaware of his official status as a murder victim, because he too spoke no Spanish.

What emerged was a grim story of drunken policemen who had beaten the Indio, until he finally agreed to put his mark on a transcript that was a complete fabrication. For the judges, the case was clear: the Indio had confessed, the Indio was guilty. They decided there was no need even to question the accused man. He was released from prison only because of the uproar that the story triggered. Those who were guilty of the miscarriage of justice, as always, preserved their jobs and suffered no punishment.

I had been to the south one other time, with Tomás, the Guatemalan singer and songwriter. He came to see me at home one day; to prepare for his arrival I stopped by El Farolito to stock up on *tacos, tortas y cerveza muy helada*. He ate in silence, as always, with his guitar on his knees. After he was done eating, he lit a cigarette and said to me:

"Max, I have to take a trip, and I don't want to go alone."

"Where do you need to go?"

"To the border."

"What border, Tomás?"

"The only border I've ever crossed in my life."

"It's dangerous, Tomás, there's a death sentence pending against you in Guatemala."

"I don't want to go into Guatemala, I only want to look at it from over the border."

"It's just as dangerous, the death squads cross the border whenever they want."

"I have to go, Max."

"Why?"

"It's my home."

"And you want me to come with you? Is that what you're asking me?"

"Yes, Max. I'd like that."

We boarded a bus run by the Estrella Blanca coach lines. We were an odd couple, two fat men—one of us white, tall, and dressed as a tourist, the other dark-skinned, short, wearing traditional dress and carrying a guitar. People looked at us, uncertain what to think. We sat side by side, our enormous asses and bellies filling the space so that it looked as if we had been born and raised aboard that bus, but we weren't uncomfortable, or perhaps I should say, we didn't pay any attention to our discomfort, because anyone who has to carry around a big awkward intrusive body like ours is accustomed to adapting to any situation. Anyway, we had so many things to talk about that the trip seemed short.

We arrived. Tomás walked toward the bridge that marked the border between the two countries. He turned off to the right and walked along beside the bridge until he found a low wall, where he sat down. I caught up with him.

"Tomás, you've been here before, haven't you?"

"I come here every year."

We pulled out of our little cooler a huge pile of fried chicken nuggets with aromatic herbs and two six packs of beer. Time went by and the shadows slowly lengthened. Including

the shadows of two fat men sitting on a low wall, intently looking across the border at Guatemala, eating, drinking, and
smoking. In complete silence.

Actually, I wanted to talk. I had thought of a number of
important questions that I wanted to ask Tomás, but clearly,
this was a moment that he wanted to experience in silence—
though I sensed that deep inside he was playing his guitar and
singing. Sweet melodies, lyrics steeped in sadness.

We polished off our food, and after a while Tomás touched
my arm: "Max."

"I'm right here, *hermano*."

"I'm getting cold. Let's go back to Mexico City."

When I heard the news of his death, I thought to myself that
he had died in a war without hope, because I had always considered the Indios to be the victims, not the protagonists of
their own history, of their own destiny.

But I was wrong. Those three old men that we interviewed
for the university had given me a rare opportunity to understand Mexico, and I let it slip through my hands, because I was
too "tainted" by my pride as a member of the European Left,
and I therefore assumed that I was culturally and politically
emancipated.

On January 1, 1994 I was at Bono, in the interior of Sardinia,
feeling stuffed after a magnificent meal of *malloreddus*, roast
suckling pig, and the powerful local grappa, *filu 'e ferru*. I was
intently playing a game of Trivial Pursuit with a group of
friends. Mexico was buried in my mind, an old and not especially pleasant memory. The television was blaring away in the
background; no one was really paying any attention. At a certain
point, however, the words "Mexico," "Chiapas," "*campesinos*,"
and "revolt" filtered through. I was suddenly glued to the
screen, watching all the international news reports.

The three old men had been right: Zapata wasn't dead at all. He had come back and was leading an army of Tojolabales, Tzotziles, and Tzeltales, Indios and *campesinos* just like him, children of the Maya, armed with rifles they usually used to hunt rabbit. The meek of the earth had declared war on the most powerful state in Central America. A war waged on behalf of agrarian land reform, a war to stop dying of hunger, measles, and diarrhea, and to abolish the privileges of the big landowners, such as the "*jus primae noctis.*" I bowed my head in grief when the television screen showed pictures of young *Zapatistas*, their hands tied behind their backs, murdered execution-style with a bullet to the back of the head. I couldn't watch; I was afraid that it might reawaken the pain and memories of the death of Tomás, killed four years earlier, just across the border.

Then I saw footage of one hundred thousand people demonstrating in Mexico City, wearing T-shirts that said "*Yo soy Zapatista,*" and after the flood of happiness, I was immediately seized by a wave of nostalgia. Nostalgia for the Mexico that I hadn't understood, and that had only done me harm, a Mexico however whose dream of revolution I loved and will always love.

The voice emerges as an echo
from the marble halls of memory
men and women pass by
as in a film

L ove and life on the run.

When I finally understood that Alessandra's words—
"Get out of my life, please, I beg you"—had swept
away the last feeble hope that this was a passing crisis and
instead marked once and for all the end of our relationship, I
was overwhelmed by the general set of sensations that one
experiences, I think, after being run over by a fast-moving
semi.

Probably, it had dawned on Alessandra that she had one last
chance to create a new life for herself. I have to admit that she
made the right decision, but in order to find the strength to
break off with me forever, she had to cut off all contact with
me and vanish literally into thin air, as far as I was concerned.

The truck hit me from behind, at the beginning of the long
road through the second phase of my battle with the courts, a
battle that went on for eight more years. Without Alessandra it
was just that much harder. It made much less sense to take on
a legal battle of that scale, a battle to regain my right to a life,
if she was no longer at my side.

Long before the truck plowed into me, I fully understood
the objective absurdity of our relationship, and how harmful it
ultimately was to her and to her life. I had talked to her about
it more than once, but I always found myself dealing with a
woman who preferred to deny there was a problem—no
doubt, unaware that she was doing so—in order to spare me
the immense pain that would inevitably ensue. Her furious

outbursts, and phrases such as "I am adult and mature enough to decide these things for myself" kept me from taking any initiative of my own, and postponed the discussion to some unspecified date in the future.

There are two things that, even now, I still find difficult to accept: her rejection of a friendship with me, and the fact that all the books, records, and other objects that documented our fifteen-year relationship vanished with her. Even things that rightly belonged to me, such as her letters and her gifts. One day she raided my house, basically, and carried everything away with her. As if she wanted to wipe away all traces. At first, I waited for her to change her mind, but she never did. Only now, after long and patient work to heal this wound, am I clear about it, and only now has the pain lessened.

The reason that I feel compelled to write about my relationship with Alessandra is the degree to which it resembles—is, indeed, identical to—the thousands of similar stories between men and women who have experienced, directly or indirectly, the world of prison and/or exile. And what these two conditions share is their powerful destructive effect upon human relationships.

A human being who is deprived of liberty or forced to flee his own country must deal with a stark and tragic set of experiences. As a result the fugitive will desperately cling to any relationship, driven not only by love but also by the need to create a minimum sense of continuity with his own past. Seen from the point of view of the other man or other woman, the situation is equally dire. Distancing and detachment are practically physiological elements in these relationships, I would venture to say, because everyday life in the end obliges them to try to safeguard their own lives. It is not selfishness, but simply the need to recognize the inevitable, after doing everything possible.

In Paris, my friends had told me right from the outset, with the wisdom inherited from a century's experience of exile, that

my relationship with Alessandra would come to an end, and
that it would be better for both of us to make a clean break as
soon as possible, in order to offer her a chance to lead a "normal life," and me an opportunity to seek out relationships
"within" the emotional universe of exile. This was good advice,
but difficult advice to accept and implement in the context of
interpersonal dynamics that refused to comply with the laws of
reason. On the one hand, of course, I felt the need to make a
decision, to choose, and on the other, I was reluctant to admin-
ister kicks in the ass to what was, after all, my own life. It was
a mistake, because long before my arrest in 1985, Alessandra
had, against her best intentions, already created a series of tensions in my mind that led me to make bad decisions, like the
final, fatal error I made in Mexico. More or less subconscious-
ly, she was laying the foundation for a final break.

I witnessed many, all too many, relationships that ultimately
ended the same way. When I think back on my own, I feel a
sense of bitterness at having lost Alessandra as a friend,
because I will never be able to tell her how much I respect and
appreciate the bravery that she showed when I was arrested in
Mexico.

Our love story began when we were both fifteen and members of the scouts. It was a beautiful, carefree time. At least,
until January 20, 1976, the day that my legal soap opera began
its long run. At the age of nineteen, I became a prison inmate
and she became a "vedova bianca."[1] She followed me from
prison to prison, showing up faithfully every visiting day; she
became a member of my own family, in part because her family—and I am referring specifically to her mother—strongly

---

[1] *Vedova bianca*: literally a "white widow," used to describe the wife of an
emigrant left behind in Italy; also used extensively in the Seventies and Eighties to describe the girlfriend or wife of a terrorist in prison or on the run
from the law.

disapproved of her relationship with a man sentenced to almost twenty years of prison.

Then I was acquitted and our love became more intense. We started to plan our life together. And then I was found guilty by the appeals court and, while awaiting the verdict of the Court of Cassation (Italy's supreme court), all our plans gave way to an intense day-to-day experience of hoping the nightmare would soon come to an end. That's not the way it went. It soon turned into a far worse nightmare: life on the run. A few months later, Alessandra came to see me in Paris and thus began her regular round of commuting, so that she was forced to live a double life, two completely different and incompatible lives. In Padua, she studied and lived at home with her family; periodically, she would meet me in some place or other in Europe, in complete secrecy. A secret, first of all, from her family, who would never have tolerated these trips of hers.

She continued to be what amounted to a "vedova bianca": even when we were together for a couple of weeks, for her it was like visiting me in prison. As a convict, I was a non-person with my non-life and no future on the horizon. After a while, she couldn't stand the double life. Padua become nothing more to her than a place to pass the time while waiting to see me again. She could no longer study (she didn't take her degree until after we broke up) or work; her folks never gave her a penny, and my parents wound up having to pay for her trips and her expenses while she was staying with me.

I soon came to realize that she too had a split existence; that she had stopped thinking about the future and was living one day at a time. When I started worrying about her and asking her serious questions about it, she lied, and spun tales of imaginary exams and promising employment opportunities.

When we were together, we forgot everything else and lived in a world all our own. We spent the days making love, strolling through the city, laughing, joking, and flirting, exchanging gifts and swearing our undying devotion. Even the security rules weren't a problem; she learned them all immediately and operated with great agility while still scrupulously obeying the laws of the underground.

Time was working against us. We were forced to deal with reality, a reality that demanded that I leave Europe. Alessandra became an enthusiastic advocate of Mexico, displaying an urgent desire for change that at first I couldn't understand, because she had hated every place we had visited so far. Just before my departure, however, when it was already too late to turn back, a discussion that began by pure chance led me to understand that she did not want to leave Padua and her family, much less to go and live with a fugitive. She loved me deeply, but she could not accept the idea of my conviction and insisted that we had to demand a new trial.

From this point of view, she got no argument from me, since the trial "was" my life and I would have paid any price to obtain justice. But at that moment, it took on a completely different meaning, practically a disassociation from the decisions we had made together; I felt all alone when I made the seventy-five-hundred-mile leap into the dark.

When the ship set sail for Veracruz, she was on the wharf, waving her scarf goodbye to me; it was a pretty scene, the sort they like to use to end romantic movies. I assumed I'd never see her again. I was wrong. She came to Mexico, but only once and for a very short visit. She found Mexico slightly revolting and very frightening. She would only talk about our legal strategy for obtaining a new trial; she avoided any other discussions about our relationship. When it was time for her to leave again, I noted that her face betrayed a slight sense of relief. But I knew I had already lost her in Paris.

When I was arrested by the Federales, my friends alerted Alessandra, who took the news to my sister. Together, they went to see my mother, who understood instantly and asked, in a tiny voice: "But he's alive, at least?"

Then Alessandra did something remarkable. She asked my family for all the cash they could raise, turned it into dollars, and took a plane to Mexico City, determined to purchase my freedom. As soon as she landed, she went straight to Calle de Soto. Fortunately, a few members of our group who were in the area spotted her and managed to stop her, hustling her away, practically kidnapping her.

Still today, when I think of the risk she ran, I get goose bumps, even though I am proud of what she did. Despite our present distance, I will never forget that last act of love, which I still consider to be one of the most significant events in my life.

After returning from Mexico, Alessandra devoted herself to the cause of the new trial until the very last. Then she disappeared. For good.

During those years, I was with other women as well. Aside from Kioko, my Japanese girlfriend in Mexico City, they were all relationships "inside the universe of exile." They were all certainly much more problematic than my relationship with Alessandra, and they were strictly short-term: a few weeks, a month, and then either she or I had something else to do, and it was over. They were good for me, I always emerged happy, refreshed, and more optimistic.

The nicest of them all was also the oddest. She was Iranian. I had met her in Madrid and then bumped into her again in Paris. I knew that she was an exile but little more. I liked her from the minute I laid eyes on her, and when I saw her intently gathering signatures against the Khomeini regime, I decided to get to know her.

"Hello, you remember me?"

"Sure, Madrid, a couple of months ago."

"What are you doing here?"

"My family moved to Paris."

"And besides collecting signatures, what do you do?"

"I work for the newspaper of my organization."

"What organization is that?"

"Mujahedeen of the Iranian People."

"*Sei tutta casa e causa?*" I asked her in Italian—roughly, "Are you all home and cause?"

"Pardon me?" she asked, eyeing me with some confusion.

"I asked what you do besides your political work."

"I'm attending a course for interpreters at a school in the Montparnasse area."

She said goodbye and went back to her work. The next day, I waited for her outside the school for interpreters. She seemed very surprised to see me.

"I couldn't resist the temptation to come pick you up after your course," I greeted her.

"What's that mean?" she asked, with a sullen, wary expression.

"That I like you and I'd like to see you more often."

That was the beginning of a long, patient courtship. I went to meet her after school, I walked her to her front door, and I participated in all of the public demonstrations against the Iranian regime, just so that I could see her.

I liked her more and more. She was a very sweet woman, intelligent, fiercely proud, with a special vein of irony that invariably targeted the status of women under Islam. I thought she was very pretty, even if her face was always wrapped in a scarf and her body was shrouded in loose flannel smocks, longer than knee-length skirts, and boots, all strictly dark brown. A color that I have always detested; I would joke with her, telling her that I had an eye disease that worsened when I had to look at dark-brown objects.

One day she asked me a series of questions about my past. Afterward, she said:

"That's a very sad story. May I tell my family about it?"

"If you like." We often talked about our childhoods, and it became a frequent pastime to tell each the other the fairy tales of our respective countries. As I walked her home, we would stop in a park, sit down on a bench together, and one of us would speak the magic words: "Once upon a time . . . "

Giggling, one day, she said to me:

"My father wants to meet you."

That made me nervous. I hastily said: "There's no hurry."

She burst into laughter: "You'll come for tea tomorrow."

"But I only drink tea when I'm sick," I objected.

I was introduced to her father, and also to her brothers. There were five of them; they all had mustaches, and they all looked at me with inscrutable expressions.

The house they lived in had belonged to her mother's family. Her mother wasn't home. I knew that her mother was French and had met her Iranian husband at the university. He was a handsome man, between sixty and seventy years old, tall and austere, with a neatly trimmed white beard.

"I had seven children, six boys and a girl," he told me, pointing to my friend, who was busy serving tea.

"Now I have only six children. The oldest boy died in Teheran prison; he was killed with the sponge torture. You know about it?"

"No."

"The war with Iraq is slaughtering our young people. The war front needs blood, for transfusions. And the Pasdaran, the revolutionary guard, takes it from political prisoners. Right down to the last drop."

"I'm very sorry . . . I had no idea."

"My children are all *mujahedeen*, and they all want to go back to Iran to fight. Even her, my only daughter."

I looked at her in surprise. She had never mentioned any of this to me, and I felt uncomfortable.

"It is a hopeless struggle. Khomeini is strong, and his strength will endure even after his death. I was a leader of Tudeh, the Iranian communist party. We believed in Khomeini's democracy, and he betrayed our trust. We no longer exist. Those who aren't dead or in prison are in exile. I am in exile for the second time; the first time I was fleeing the regime of the Shah. Now my children all want to fight on the Iraqi side. Many other young people are already at the front."

I broke in: "I understand your bitterness. But I don't understand why you're telling me about all this."

"You are courting my daughter, and this I don't like. From what she has told me, you are wanted as a criminal in your own land and this I like even less. My sons will leave us, and my wife and I will be all alone. I have some hopes of persuading my daughter not to squander her life pointlessly, so in the meanwhile, would you please leave her alone? I ask you this as a courtesy, our family needs tranquility."

"That's your daughter's decision," I replied, and walked to the door.

The next day, I went to wait for her outside her school as usual. I felt sad, not so much because of what her father had said to me, but because learning about the tragic situation of her family had swept away the beauty and innocence of our relationship.

"Why didn't you ever tell me about your family? Why wait for your father to do it?"

"Are you mad at me?" she asked.

"No, but I feel as if I've been wounded by another tragedy, as if destiny had decided to force me to look at all the horror in the world. I'm not strong enough for that. Maybe your father is right, maybe I'm the least appropriate person to be close to you. Anyway, I don't even know whether or not you like me. Before I met your father and your silent brothers, our friendship was a breath of fresh air. Now, instead, I sense the looming presence of a story, a history that doesn't belong to me, and choices that I want no part of."

"I liked you better when you told me fairy tales," she said, with a sly air. "You want to know what my mother told me? She told me that the time has come for me to go to your house."

She was much prettier than I expected. As she undressed, there emerged a twenty-four-year-old woman with raven hair and silken skin. The most beautiful woman I've ever seen. I plunged into her eyes, endlessly lost, until the day she told me: "My brothers are leaving soon."

"What about you?"

"I'm staying."

"I'm glad. You made the right decision."

"My boyfriend is here now."

"I thought I was your boyfriend," I joked.

"He was in Germany, now he's moved to Paris."

"Then we won't see each other again. I'll be the first to say it. It had to happen, I know that; I'm not sad about it. It's been a beautiful thing. The only thing I regret is that we didn't start making love the first day we met . . . "

"Not me. I liked being courted by such a gallant Italian gentleman," she said, laughing.

"You watch out for yourself."

"You too."

RETURN

My gaze
is a crystal
focusing back over the years

M y return from Mexico marked the beginning of the legal battle to win a new trial. That battle engaged the passions of a great portion of public opinion both in Italy and around the world. Committees of Solidarity were formed in various Italian cities; there was also an international Solidarity Committee with offices in Paris and London.

After a series of lengthy interlocutory motions and countermotions before the Appeals Court of Venice, on June 20, 1988, my panel of defense lawyers submitted a petition for a new trial to the Court of Cassation, the highest court of appeal.

In the meanwhile, in November 1987, I was released from prison *per differimento pena*, or deferment of sentence, a legal formula that refers to a temporary suspension of incarceration to give an inmate an opportunity to obtain medical treatment. I could not accept imprisonment or the verdict, and I sought escape in an unprecedented bout of bulimia. My metabolism altered so radically that I became especially at risk for strokes and heart attacks. The Supervisory Court decided to allow me my first eight months of conditional release. Those eight months were then extended repeatedly because my health never improved to an acceptable level.

In January 1989, the Court of Cassation ruled in favor of a new trial, overturning the lower court's judgment of conviction and sending the case to the Appeals Court of Venice for a new judgment.

On October 20th of the same year, four days (a gap that

would prove fatal) before the new code of criminal procedure entered into effect, my new trial began. It ended on December 22, 1990. The court, after fourteen months of preliminary investigatory hearings, failed to hand down a judgment. Instead, it issued an interlocutory decree, sending the case to the Constitutional Court for instructions as to which criminal procedure it should apply. The court had come to a final judgment of acquittal for insufficient evidence, but it had run headlong into the following dilemma: if the old code of criminal procedure were applied, then the accused should be found guilty, but under the new code of criminal procedure, there should be a full acquittal.

My case was sent back to Rome, to be heard by the Constitutional Court which decided, on July 5, 1991, in an interpretative opinion, that the Venetian court had committed a serious judicial error by ignoring the transitory provisions, which required, in cases of this sort, that the accused be unconditionally acquitted.

The court record was bundled up and shipped back to Venice, where the Appeals Court was expected to reconvene and retire to chambers for five full minutes of deliberation; sufficient time to write a new opinion and pronounce its judgment of acquittal.

In the meantime, however (the wheels of justice don't exactly spin at dizzying speed), the Chief Judge of the court, which had carefully considered my case for fourteen whole months, had celebrated his birthday, reached legal retirement age, and was now enjoying his pension. On February 21, 1992, (the date set for the new hearing by the Appeals Court) I found myself facing a new Chief Judge and a completely different panel of judges. That panel, exercising its right to autonomous judgment, chose to skip the preliminary judicial investigation (which was replaced by a summary reading of the proceedings), and in the course of just a few hearings, on March 27, issued a new opinion that reconfirmed the guilty verdict and eighteen-year sentence first handed down in 1979. A firing squad.

The following day, just twenty-four hours after the judgment, with truly unusual rapidity, the State Attorney's office issued an arrest warrant, and once again I wound up in prison. All of this took place in an atmosphere of almost universal astonishment and dismay, because in the history of Italian justice, it had never before happened that a convict, with a penalty deferred for reasons of health by the only institute with jurisdiction to do so, that is, the Supervisory Court, should be incarcerated without a specific order to that effect issued by that Supervisory Court.

Back in prison, I sank into a hopeless state of abulia and bulimia. In other, simpler words, I was stuffing myself like a Christmas goose while displaying an unsettling indifference to everything around me. My health worsened rapidly, and after forty-seven days of hearings and medical examinations, the consulting psychiatrist named by the Supervisory Court issued this finding: "Unless you would like to read his obituary in the newspaper in the next few days, you need to release him." At that point, I was given one year's provisional liberty. This was also partly the result of the indignant reaction of public opinion. There was a groundswell of support, prompted by my reconviction and arrest, for the new campaign undertaken by the "Massimo Home Now" Committees.

My case records were shipped back to Rome, where they were set before the Court of Cassation; but the judgment was practically a foregone conclusion. In fact, on November 24, 1992, a hasty hearing put an end once and for all to the Carlotto Case.

The court ordered me to return to prison on May 13, 1993, where I could plan on remaining, paying my debt to society until the year 2004.

In that final phase of my legal soap opera, between the end of March 1992 and April 7, 1993, the day I was given a presidential pardon, the idea of life on the run once again became a distinct possibility. Not a single journalist I talked to failed to ask if I was planning to escape, once again, as the last way out of prison and an unjust conviction.

In all honesty, I replied that the idea had not even passed through my head, but I had to admit that the question was not unreasonable. The legal outcome had been turned on its head. An acquittal that had been announced and recommended by the Constitutional Court had been replaced, with all the speed of a magic act, by a conviction. After seventeen years, eleven trials, and a legal battle fought down to the last writ, I found myself looking at twelve years in prison, an extremely fragile mental and physical condition, and—worst of all—an infamous accusation, and conviction, that I had never, after all this time, been able to accept.

Anyone could do the math. The sentence was eighteen years; I had already served six, which left twelve. Add the twelve years to the seventeen that the entire matter had already taken from me, and you had a total of almost thirty years of my life locked up in this case. An absurd number, which led many people to urge me to flee; not my friends from the committees of solidarity, of course, but people I ran into on the street, in cafés, at newsstands. They would walk up to me, shake my hand, and after a few conventional phrases, lean forward and whisper: "Run away, you're sick, you'll only die in prison, you've already suffered enough . . . "

I couldn't help but feel grateful for their solidarity, but I responded to everyone that I would never do it. It was a decision that I had already made the day after the judgment of the Appeals Court, and I had explained it at great length to a reporter from the *Corriere della Sera* in an interview I granted just a few hours prior to my arrest.

So here we were, talking about life on the run again, but this was an idea that I rejected for a number of reasons. First of all, to run would have been a betrayal of the trust of all those citizens who believed in my legal battle. Second, it would have been a betrayal of the trust of the Supervisory Court, which had ordered my release from prison to safeguard my health, not to facilitate my escape from the law. Among other considerations, I couldn't ignore the fact that if I ran, the result would be the rejection of similar requests from other sick inmates, because, in Italy, an individual's penal responsibility, once inserted in a prison context, is no longer limited to the individual, but extends to the entire prison population. Last of all, I didn't want to give any comfort to the small but powerful faction of those who believed I was guilty, and I knew they would have a field day if I escaped, pointing to the fact as proof of my guilt.

In other words, running away would be meaningless. If, in the past, escape had served to delegitimate the judgment of conviction, that judgment—after seventeen years and eleven trials—had emptied itself of meaning. If the idea of avoiding the penalty was meaningless, there was even less meaning in the idea of returning voluntarily to prison, because it would have been tantamount to an unconditional surrender, not only to the final judgment, but in the ultimate analysis to everything that had happened in all those years.

I found myself in a complex situation. On the one hand, I did not want to run, and on the other, I didn't want to go back to prison. There was still the chance of a pardon, but at the time it looked like an extremely remote possibility. I had always stated publicly that I would never ask for a pardon because I was innocent and, under the Italian system, one of the conditions of granting a pardon is an admission of guilt and a corresponding repentance. Since there was no precedent of a pardon given without an admission of guilt, it struck me as impossible to obtain.

Neither escape nor prison; that was my basic policy. What, then, was to be done? While I was sifting my thoughts in search of a solution, my family, my team of defense lawyers, and the Solidarity Committees decided to request a pardon on my behalf. My parents submitted a formal appeal, through the defense lawyers, to the Appeals Court with jurisdiction over the matter, and the matter began to wend its way through the bureaucratic labyrinth. The Solidarity Committees, on the other hand, held a press conference, in order to give the consulting jurists an opportunity to present the campaign in support of the initiative, which called for the circulation of a petition to be presented to the President of the Republic when a sufficient number of signatures had been gathered.

At first, I found myself all alone, for the first time, in opposition to all those who loved me or were supporting my cause. I was by no means opposed to the idea of a pardon (in fact, I viewed it as the only instrument available to rectify and render equitable the harsh rigors of the law, the only tool capable of closing the case with justice and humanity), but my complete certainty that the appeal would be rejected led me to believe that my family, lawyers, and Solidarity Committees were launching into a hopeless venture.

My counterproposal was this: let's focus all our energy on the lawsuit I had already brought against the Italian state for its repeated violations, to my personal harm and detriment, of the European Convention on Human Rights and Fundamental Freedoms, which fell under the jurisdiction of the Strasbourg Court of Human Rights. The general response was that, while that lawsuit was certainly important, their main interest was to keep me from being sent back to prison, which would be an act of injustice that would undoubtedly lead to my death, considering the steady deterioration of my own state of health.

We slowly came to a laborious compromise: I would collaborate and take part in every initiative in favor of a pardon, and

I would support the principle of justice intrinsic to the issue of a pardon, but I would also insist on making it clear that I, as the defendant, had never asked for a pardon myself, because I was innocent.

And so an extraordinary groundswell of support swept across Europe, a grassroots campaign in favor of my pardon. Eminent jurists, leading figures in the worlds of culture and the arts, politicians and ordinary citizens mobilized to put an end to the longest running case in the history of Italian justice. They did everything possible—and impossible.

I have memories of that time that are at once terrible and magnificent; terrible because of the state of anxiety and tension that grew in me, day by day, as the final deadline of May 13th drew closer; magnificent because of the intense human warmth of that groundswell of support. I traveled throughout Italy, taking part in a dizzying array of events, initiatives, press conferences, panel discussions, and performances; and everywhere I went I was swept up in an overwhelming wave of warmth and affection from so many people.

Around the middle of February, just three months away from the deadline of May 13th, the slowness of the bureaucratic labyrinth forced me to make a reality check. Based on my own personal experience of seventeen years of dealing with the "pace" of justice, I felt certain that my request would never make it to the desk of the Minister of Justice in time, much less to the desk of the President of the Republic. The general political climate of Italy at that juncture was also less than promising, and I couldn't envision the Minister and the President finding the time to sit down and study such a complex case.

It was different now, admittedly. There had been an unprecedented mobilization of public opinion, and there could be no mistaking the fact that my case was unique. I thought the odds were a little better, but time was still against me. I thought things over carefully, and came to the conclusion that I could not change my stance. I would refuse to run away, and I would refuse to go back to prison.

Neither escape nor prison. What else was to be done?

I could feel myself getting angrier and angrier. I saw that once again nothing but an act of stark refusal could make it unmistakably clear that I would never, never accept "that judgment" and "that sentence," handed down by "that system of justice."

A justice made up of "ifs." If the trial hadn't begun four days before the new code of criminal procedure came into effect, if the court hadn't been plagued by doubts, if the judges had been properly informed about the transitory provisions and their proper interpretation (they should have been; it was their duty to be), if the chief justice hadn't retired . . . if only all these things, then I wouldn't have been found guilty, I wouldn't have been sentenced to prison; I would have been acquitted and set free.

A prominent and respected magistrate of the Italian Republic said, in this connection, that this was a case of "jinxed justice." He was probably right, but how can justice be jinxed?

And that wasn't all. Because the Chief Justice of the Appeals Court had retired, I had been subjected to two different trials at the same level of appeals. A unique case, never to be repeated—but doesn't it say in every courtroom in Italy that the law is equal for all?

And, again, is it acceptable or even conceivable that a trial that stretched on for fourteen full months, with the examination and cross-examination of witnesses and the careful sifting and investigation of expert analyses, counted for less than another trial that was over after a few hearings, and which consisted of a simple reading of the minutes and documents? There might be a technical explanation for it, but how does it square with the most elementary concept of justice?

Eight judges—two magistrates and six civilian members of

the panel, roughly speaking, jurors—had read the court documents and handed down a judgment of guilty; five more judges—all magistrates—said that there were no legal defects in their verdict, and the case was closed, once and for all.

Dozens of jurists and many, many magistrates had looked at the same documents, and they had all concurred that I was innocent and that there had been a terrible miscarriage of justice. So where, then, was the certain proof of my guilt, in the face of such conflicting judgments? And that's leaving aside the mistaken expert witnesses, the blundered investigations, the missing evidence, the length of the preventive detention, the arbitrary nature of the special prison, and the illness caused by incarceration.

"Enough," I thought to myself, "no more." I decided that the time had come to take arms against the slings and arrows of an inhuman system of justice. The only tool left to me, the only form of rebellion against the enormity of the injustices being visited up me, was my own life. So if a pardon wasn't issued by May 13th, I would renounce that life.

I had never considered suicide before; in fact, my human and ideological belief system led me to consider it as a form of surrender. But it was the only option left open to me as a way of preserving the last shreds of my personal dignity, the only handle on my own life that justice had not been able to snatch away. I had no desire to end my life. But suicide, in that context, had the value of an act of war against my judges—magistrates and jurors of the Venice Appeals Court—whom I blamed as the chief villains behind everything that had happened to me.

"They behaved like a firing squad; let them be a firing squad then," I said to myself. I resented them for finding me guilty, but especially for my absolute certainty that they were only superficially familiar with the documents of the case. I was devastated when I read their opinion and found an astonishing number of errors and inaccuracies. But the straw that broke the camel's back was in the last lines of the verdict. It was this phrase: "with this judgment of conviction, the Court wishes to make the 'Carlotto case' a worthy episode in Italian judicial history."

I had no other option. There were no more legal tools to challenge their truth. I needed to up the ante, and this time the bet was going to be my life.

In this perspective, I believed that a pardon, if it were granted before May 13th, would acquire the unmistakable stamp of an act of justice and humanity, arriving as it would in so timely and unusual a manner. Especially because the Venice Court of Appeals had expressed the opposite view. A pardon, then, was still within the realm of hope, and I clutched desperately at that elusive hope. Still, I had to have the tough-minded, clear-eyed discipline to face the likelihood of suicide.

And so I set off for another brisk hike through the landscape of madness, a trek that would last ninety days or so. In fact, from the point of view of everyday logic, the reasoning that had led me to such a radical, uncompromising decision absolutely shattered into a thousand pieces; but within the framework of the whole experience, it looked rigorous and unassailable.

The thing that, more than anything else, convinced me to overcome my hesitations and set busily about organizing the "event" was the mental picture of me emerging from prison at the ripe old age of forty-eight and saying to myself: "All right then, time to rebuild my life."

Convinced that suicide can't be improvised (the world is teeming with pitiful dilettantes who annoy their fellow humans with tiresome explanations of why they failed in the attempt), I took pen and paper and set down a list of problems to be resolved.

Problem number one: the means. Of course, I wanted it to

be quick and painless. Leafing through books of forensic medicine and asking, with a totally apathetic, clueless air, extremely specific questions of the people I considered to be experts in
the field, I soon came to prefer a massive and carefully blended dose of drugs. I soon had all the fixings.

I divided them into two boxes. One box contained the
drugs that would cause my death. I would take them first, and
so, to avoid any confusion, I marked the box with a large number "1." The other box, it goes without saying, was marked
with a number "2"—written in indelible marker—and it contained the drugs I would gulp down immediately after the
lethal dose. They would render me unconscious just long
enough for the first dose of drugs to do its work. It seemed like
a lot of pills, and I was concerned that I might not manage to
get them all down. I certainly didn't want my suicide attempt
to fail because I had overlooked any minor details, so I went to
a candy store and bought a bag of sweets that were about the
same shape and size as the pills I would be taking. I ran a couple of test sessions and determined that I would have no problem swallowing that number of capsules, as long as I took care
to avoid washing them down with a carbonated beverage.

Which brought me to the second problem: the place. It took
more time and effort to solve that one than I expected. The
most important determining factor was this: I didn't want it to
happen in the jurisdiction of the Padua Coroner's Office. To
put it in stark terms, the last thing that I wanted was to be
brought face to face, especially when I was dead, with the
physical remains and other evidence that had vanished so mysteriously during the trial. It would have been too much for me.

Of course, since I didn't want to cause my relatives and my
friends any extra pain, I ruled out their houses from the very
start. I also excluded hotels and public places in general, out of
a sense of etiquette and good taste. There were a few places
that met all my requirements, but which just might lead the

usual boneheads into a series of elaborate theories in search of some deep hidden meaning. After time-consuming scouting expeditions, I finally found a lovely place in the mountains that was perfect. I traveled the route several times, and explored and identified a few alternative routes, just in case the road was blocked that day by a wreck or a repair crew.

Then I went on to plan the trickiest part: making sure that the timing of the "event" and its subsequent discovery would match up with the timing of the mass media. I didn't want the news of my suicide to get out before the press got its hands on the forty-page document that I had written to explain the reasons for my act.

This forced me to move my planning ahead by two days, because I didn't feel that I could rely on the reckoning of dates by the person issuing the arrest warrant. The way I figured it, if I began my count on the 14th, the one year would be up on May 13th; but the court officer might begin on May 13th, which would mean that the year expired on the 12th. And so, in order to make sure that the news of the warrant for my arrest and the reports of my demise would coincide, I decided to add a margin of safety.

Since, as the saying goes, hope springs eternal, I'll admit that I wasn't happy about moving up the date; I knew that fate liked to bedevil me, and I was worried that I might kill myself on the 11th and then find myself, a stupefied invisible spirit (I couldn't get the angels from *Wings of Desire* out of my head), standing beside the President of the Republic on the 12th as he signed the request for a pardon, unable to tell him that he really needn't bother.

To make things worse, I had plenty of experience with the justice system's grasp of basic arithmetic; I wasn't wrong to worry. Here's just one example (I could think of plenty more): my height. According to the city hall of records, according to me, and according to the many physicians who have measured my height, I am 186 centimeters tall. The justice system, on the other hand, says I am 182 centimeters tall, and there was nothing that I could do to persuade them otherwise. Once, a group of six experts measured me in every way imaginable, and when I realized that they had me down as four centimeters shorter than my actual height, I pointed out their error. They just looked at me with an incinerating glare. And ever since that day, if someone asks me how tall I am, I have to give a two-part answer: "Well, according to the hall of records, six foot one, but forensically, five eleven and a half because, you see . . . "

To come back to the media, what mattered most to me was to ensure that, by the time the news of my death was reported, the press had all had time to read my forty-page document, so that nobody would be left in doubt or be able to put a self-interested spin on my suicide.

I wished I could have made it shorter but, aside from the fact that I've never been good at being brief, it really wasn't easy to condense more than seventeen years of events, along with accompanying explanations and legal arguments. Moreover, I wanted to take full advantage of my impending status as a newsworthy dead person to write all the things that I'd never been able to say while alive, for fear of ruining my chances in court. And it had taken a few pages.

When a person decides to commit suicide, he should start by calculating exactly how many personal letters he'll have to write in order to give an explanation of his "act of tragic desperation." If I had realized I would have to write one hundred seventy-three letters, I would probably have lost heart and just decided to make it look like an accident. But by now, the planning had gone too far.

Still, I have a lot of friends, and I wanted to bid a proper farewell to each of them. It was quite a task, especially during a period of feverish activity on behalf of the pardon. It forced me into a sort of clandestine world, because I had to write in secret and then skillfully conceal the letters in the oddest places imaginable.

There was another, not inconsequential aspect of this period: I was already basically dying anyway because of how far out of whack my metabolism had gone; all of my readings were off the charts. I was constantly on the brink of a stroke or a myocardial infarction, and angina attacks were daily occurrences. My bodily organs were all grinding to a halt, day by day. I could distinctly feel the sensation of my organs losing touch with one another. It was a weird feeling, as if I had suddenly grown old. An infinite weariness was bringing me to my knees and even the smallest task took an enormous effort.

One evening, an attack that persisted despite the Diltrate that I gulped down threw me into a state of panic; I hurried to the hospital, afraid I was about to die. I couldn't let that happen, because I wasn't ready yet, and it was the wrong day.

Back at home the next day, my mother looked oddly at me and said: "Son, when you were in the hospital, you said a series of things I didn't understand. You talked about an 'event,' a document for the press that you needed to finish, eighty letters left to write. What were you talking about?"

Here was a whole new problem: I might simply drop dead before the 11th, and there was nothing I could do about that. But according to my doctors, the brain damage caused by a stroke could result in paralysis. I could wind up in a wheelchair or even worse, lying in a bed somewhere, in a coma, my tongue dangling out of the side of my mouth.

The idea of facing trial in a wheelchair, glassy-eyed and slack-jawed, was the most frightening thing I could imagine. I decided to speak to an ex-con with whom for a long time I had shared a 120-square foot cell, toilet and sink included. He was a good friend, a tough guy who had seen it all. I went to see him and I said: "You need to swear that if I ever have a stroke and turn into a zombie and can't even wipe my ass, you'll help me kill myself." He looked at me with the detached interest you might expect from an entomologist: "Let me see if I understand you here. You're asking me to swear that, if you have a stroke and go into a coma or whatever, I'll ice you. Have you lost it?"

"If it happened to you, you'd ask me the same thing. You're over fifty, you're starting to be the right age for that sort of thing." Superstitiously grabbing his nuts, he answered: "You're right, I've spent too much time in jail to become a paralytic. But would you do the same for me?"

"Not a chance!"

"Nice friend you turn out to be. So why should I do it for you?"

"Because you owe me a lot of favors. Want me to refresh your memory?"

"Don't remind me. Okay, you have a deal. How do you want it done? I can't just walk into the hospital and shoot you in the head."

"No, I've already thought it through," I answered. "You get yourself some LSD and slip a few tabs under my tongue. That'll take care of it."

"Acid? That's for druggies, you know I never got involved in that stuff. Listen, here's a better idea, I'll slip a plastic bag over your head . . . "

"For Christ's sake," I interrupted him, "are you looking to go to prison? Acid is the best way, they'll just think I had a heart attack. I read about this in a book about forensic medicine."

"Okay, if you say so, acid it is."

We shook hands and I kissed his cheek in the standard Italian convict ceremony of a binding promise: "Thanks, you're a pal. Now don't worry about it, I can almost guarantee you that you won't have to do this thing."

"Let's hope not." And then he added, "No offense, but you seemed less out-of-your-mind when you were in jail."

*

I decided to finish my planning for the "event" and end my involvement in the campaign for the pardon at the end of March. I wanted to have at least a month (for the first time in many years) just for myself.

In just three months, over eighteen thousand signatures had been gathered (with a great number of illustrious names), panel discussions had been organized, along with concerts, shows, and television and radio programs. The media, in general, were rooting for the pardon. In brief, things looked good, but everyone also realized that the odds of obtaining an answer before May 13th were slender at best.

In a generally demoralized meeting, the Committees agreed to organize a national moblilization day on March 26th, with the slogan "Forty-Eight Days to Pardon Massimo Carlotto," a continuation of the campaign even after my imminent arrest, and a general effort to convince me to prepare for another stretch in prison.

At the same time, a campaign to urge me to escape sprang back into life. Among those who came to see me was a group of friends I hadn't seen for years. They begged me to run.

The smart money was on me staying. In Padua, the official odds were against my escaping, and bets were being taken at a good clip. Every so often, I would get a phone call from a stranger asking how things were going with request for a pardon, and advising me not to do anything hasty.

I chose the date of March 26th for my last public appearance. Among the many scheduled gatherings, I chose to attend a performance/happening in a theater in Padua. The main reason I went was so that I could say goodbye to many dear friends, including most of the artists on the bill that night.

Before the actual show, there were a series of speeches. One speech, by a woman named Kissi, of the Milan Committee, gave an eloquent presentation of the anguish experienced by all those who were fighting for my pardon, and who feared that pardon wouldn't come before May. She said:

"I've spent a lot of time thinking about the things that make me feel angry, helpless, and indignant. We are all victims of the government to some degree. I have been waiting for payments from the state for three years now. I no longer seem to have a right to my own health care. And a terrible rage begins to build up. The people who are supposed to look out for you are busy picking your pockets. But these are all marginal issues in my life, or at least I can set them aside. I can 'tune them out,' if I try. But Carlotto can't ignore his. With any understanding of the terrible things that have happened to him, none of us can feel safe. Who will protect us? To my mind, we can only depend on ourselves, on the 'voice of the public.'

"Let's band together. Let's step out of the silence of our homes. Let's all raise our voices as one. If you can speak, speak in public. If you can write, you must write. If you can paint, then paint.

"Remember: there are only forty-eight days left to win this pardon. Write, even if you only write letters of outrage to the newspapers. And another thing: Massimo is an unusual convict: no tears, no yelling, no complaints. He is restrained, but most of all, he is intelligent and tenacious, and they hate that. Only if the voice of the public becomes a mighty avalanche will Massimo be safe.

"If he is pardoned, an innocent Massimo Carlotto will nevertheless be considered by the state a guilty man set free, regardless of the facts of his case. This too is a source of outrage for us. The state owes Massimo Carlotto seventeen years of human and civil rights; at least let's try to save his life."

When it was over, I hugged everyone and said goodbye. The next day, I boarded a plane for Cagliari. I intended to stay in

Sardinia for about a month, and then come home to spend my last few days with my family.

I had chosen Sardinia because there I would be able to enjoy the company of the sea, the sun, and so many close friends. I still remember my sense of euphoria at the idea that I would finally be able to devote some time to myself, free of court-imposed deadlines. The tension was still palpable, of course, and the days ticked off inexorably, but I had made my decision. I was ready. Let fate take its course. I felt a great wave of peace sweep over me: for the first time, I could look at the world around me. For all those years, I had been witness, suspect, detainee, defendant; and then acquitted, convicted, hunted, imprisoned and released on grounds of illness, re-accused, re-acquitted, re-convicted, re-imprisoned and re-released on grounds of illness. Now I was going to try to get away from all that, try to be something else, perhaps not quite myself but something similar, a little less dehumanized, a little less "Carlotto case."

I drew up a short list of the books, records, and movies that would keep me company for that month. During the day, I was always alone, but solitude was no longer an enemy; now it was a space within me through which I moved with an unaccustomed lightness, enjoying even the most insignificant things. I spent the nights with my friends, feasting and drinking, rediscovering the fun of laughter, the idle excitement of reckless gossip. I slipped into bed moderately drunk; sleep hurried in and embraced me faithfully till morning.

But I couldn't stave off my past. The dialogue in a book, a scene in a movie, the melody of a song kept taking me back. At first, I tried to resist, but then I let my mind roam free, and it would dig up and fetch even the tiniest, most insignificant memories back to me. I was tired of feeling emotions, and I wandered the paths of memory with a sense of detachment. I no longer even felt like asking questions, seeking answers.

From time to time, I wondered if it had been worth suffering for almost half my life.

Dead or pardoned, the Carlotto case was about to come to an end, once and for all, and I decided to celebrate the event appropriately by selecting and honoring the funniest comment on the trial. Not an easy task, considering the number of excellent candidates. In the end, however, the award went to the mother of a friend who said to me, with great empathy and in all seriousness: "Let's hope they let you off . . . at least with a reserved prognosis."

I sent her a bouquet, with my anonymous gratitude. It was the only thing worth remembering out of the whole affair.

In some ways, I couldn't wait for the moment of truth to arrive; there was something asinine and annoying about the ostensible detachment with which I was approaching the wait that made it unbearable. I found myself mulling over saccharine anecdotes and embroidering on the way certain events had turned out, and how they had influenced my life. All things that had no meaning for me now. But I couldn't resist the temptation to attribute a ritual significance to the wait. I started to hate myself. I told myself that I had never been so obscenely tiresome and quarrelsome, and then I'd try not to be so hard on myself . . . After all, I did have some justification.

Wednesday, April 7, 1993. It was a little after eleven when I woke up. The chemical imbalance in my metabolism immediately demanded a shot of nicotine; I dragged myself, dressed in boxer shorts, to the living room, hunting for my cigarettes and my lighter, using my hands, more than my eyes. "Thirty-four days to go," I thought, but it meant nothing to me, and I shoved the idea aside. I put on my sunglasses and went out onto the balcony to smoke a second cigarette. My elbows propped on the railing, my gaze ranged out, focusing first on the almond grove, then the pond, and then the sea. Every so often, a flock of pink flamingoes would flap into the air. "Looking for food," I thought, and my appetite awoke. I got dressed and headed downstairs to the pastry shop at a leisurely pace. A glass of iced tea to soothe my throat, scorched from too many cigarettes and too much grappa the night before, then a cappuccino and a few sweet buns. The crumbs dribbled onto the local newspaper spread out on the café table; slowly, to keep from losing my place as I read, I swept them to the edge of the page, letting them fall to the floor.

With the bundle of newspapers under my arm, I walked over to the wine shop, where the proprietor welcomed me with the greeting he reserved for those special customers who appreciated his selection of wines and liquors. The metallic taste in my mouth called for a full-bodied white, with a pungent herby nose, so I chose a sauvignon and a gewürztraminer.

It was warming up; walking in the hot sunshine made me want to head home, but I still needed to drop by the video store to rent a couple of movies for the long afternoon that lay ahead of me.

It was almost one o'clock when I hurriedly opened the front door and rushed to answer the insistently ringing phone. As I grabbed the receiver, I heard the answering machine click on and, before I could say hello, I had to wait for the recorded outgoing message to end.

"This is a message for Massimo Carlotto, this is his lawyer . . ."

I broke in: "Ciao, this is Massimo, is there news?"

"It's done!" he yelled into the phone. "You've been pardoned."

I hung up after mumbling a few incomprehensible words and sat down on the sofa, trying to feel some emotion, anything. I felt nothing: only my body seemed to have been affected by the news, developing a slight tremor, especially my hands and right leg.

I walked back out onto the balcony and propped my elbows

on the railing again, lighting my thousandth cigarette. The almond grove, the pond, the pink flamingoes, and the sea, motionless in the hottest hour of the day, were all testifying their absolute indifference to the positive conclusion of the longest legal proceeding in Italian history.

I stood staring until the cigarette burned down to the end, scorching my fingers. "Maybe I should stop smoking," I thought to myself, sucking on them to soothe the pain.

It'll snow again this year
in my mind, it's already freezing
autumn used to be good and cozy and warm, but not anymore
all told, this biting cold just makes me feel old . . .

The pardon was a sterling development. Now it's all over. I no longer have to defend myself from anyone, and my delirious encounters with persecution and death are safely in the past.

If I want to go out and buy a pack of cigarettes, I no longer have to make sure that I am accompanied by two witnesses and a lawyer to keep from being framed. I just give them a quick phone call to let them know I'm going out.

I never sleep alone. I take a Ray-Ban-wearing plush duck to bed with me. I bought it so Ramón would have company when he comes to see me in my dreams.

In order finally to occupy my time in some socially useful fashion, I planned to found the Society for Veteran Accidental Fugitives (the S.V.A.F.), with a walk-in clinic to help members in trouble. My lawyers paternally advised against the idea; they tell me it would be illegal.

This is a strange country we live in. Veterans of Gladio— Italy's secret, subversive, NATO-sponsored, post-WWII, anti-Communist "stay-behind" army—founded an association and no one put them in prison. Don't try to tell me that an accidental fugitive is capable of more mischief than a deranged patriot who hides assault weapons and TNT in his grandmother's burial vault.

I am struggling with a nasty, obnoxious diet, and the pounds are melting away, perhaps for good.

I must have missed something over the past few years,

because everything seems different. Even the borders have changed. Last summer, with my brand new (and most important, authentic) passport, I crossed the borders of half of Europe. I would pull up to the customs station, my body half out of the car window, frantically waving the passport to catch a guard's attention. No one even looked at it; at some of the border crossings, there weren't even guards anymore. I guess I'll have to resign myself to the idea that I did my living on the run during the most difficult part of the postwar years.

People tell me I can finally start a new life. I don't know about that. I look around and I don't like what I see. In fact, it fills me with a healthy dose of anxiety, which inevitably turns into cosmic laziness.

I think I'll wait for Silvia Baraldini to come home from her imprisonment in the United States before dedicating myself to the future.

By the way, we do what we can to help Silvia, sweet unsinkable rebel that she is, but it's never enough. Indignation swells, but it hasn't worked yet. Maybe if we shut down the bakeries of Italy, that would force the government to put its foot down and "demand" that she be brought back home. I can't stop thinking about it. Every day.

Maybe that's why I have a strange dream from time to time. I'm on a plane, flying to Memphis with a group of Sardinian musicians, friends of mine; they have a band called the Nonpartisans. We have a plan. Occupy Elvis Presley's mansion. Later in that same dream, we've occupied Graceland and, while the Nonpartisans "desecrate" the temple of rock 'n' roll with Afro-Sardinian-Caribbean rhythms, my face appears on television (CNN, of course). Staring straight ahead, I threaten to use a sledgehammer to destroy the legendary Elvis Presley's favorite guitar if the government of the United States refuses to release Silvia Baraldini immediately. In the last part of the dream, we're flying back to Italy. My friends are still playing. My gaze shifts away slightly, and meets her big, pale-blue eyes.

It's a nice dream, but when I wake up, I always feel even more depressed than before. I don't know what to do. So I wait.

While waiting, I suppose I could engage in a few séances; I've been wanting to get in touch with Edward Hopper, rest his soul, and ask him to paint me into *Nighthawks*. He's my favorite artist. "Entering into" his paintings over these past difficult years has saved my imagination from extinction.

I'd like to be leaning on the counter in that 1942 diner, between the coffee machine and the redhead.

Silent, sober as a judge, waiting for the night to end.

1994

---

* On September 26, 2006, Silvia Baraldini was freed as a result of a general amnesty.

PUBLISHER'S NOTE
This appendix provides a chronology
of Massimo Carlotto's legal saga.

On January 20, 1976, a twenty-five-year-old university student named Margherita Magello was murdered in her home in Padua, with fifty-nine stab wounds.

Massimo Carlotto, age nineteen, a university student and a militant in the left-wing protest group Lotta Continua, happened upon the victim, bloodied and on the verge of death. He went to a Carabiniere station to report what had happened. He was detained, placed under arrest, and charged with murder.

On May 5, 1978, Massimo Carlotto, after over a year of preliminary investigation and following three trials (the first ended in a ruling ordering additional forensic examinations and further investigation, the second was adjourned due to illness of the Chief Judge), he was acquitted for insufficient evidence by the trial court in Padua.

On December 19, 1979 the Venice Court of Appeals overturned the acquittal and sentenced Massimo Carlotto to eighteen years in prison.

On November 19, 1982 the Court of Cassation declined to hear the defense's appeal and upheld the verdict.

On February 2, 1985 Massimo Carlotto returned to Italy from Mexico and turned himself over to the Italian authorities.

During that same year, the Comité International Justice pour Massimo Carlotto was founded, with offices in Padua, Rome, Paris, and London. The committee began a media campaign and circulated a petition in favor of a new trial. Thousands of signatures were gathered. The first signature in Italy was that of Norberto Bobbio, the philosopher and Senator-for-Life. Internationally, the first signature was that of the Brazilian writer Jorge Amado, who issued an international appeal for a new trial in June 1986. The appeal appeared in the pages of *Le Monde* and was endorsed by dozens of other respected intellectuals.

In the meantime, Massimo Carlotto became seriously ill in prison, and a new campaign for his release was initiated.

In February 1987, the International Federation for Human Rights began an investigation of the Carlotto case, and sent a commission to Padua, headed by the federation's secretary general, Patrick Baudoin. Following an examination of the court records and interviews with the various parties, the federation called for a new trial.

On November 12, 1987, following a series of medical examinations and hearings before the Supervisory Court, Massimo Carlotto obtained an order of deferment of sentence due to serious health problems.

On June 20, 1988, Carlotto's defense team, after a series of lengthy interlocutory motions and countermotions before the Court of Appeals in Venice, submitted a petition for a new trial to the Court of Cassation, the highest court of appeal.

On January 30, 1989, the Court of Cassation ruled in favor of a new trial on the strength of three new items of evidence. It thus overturned the lower court's judgment of conviction and sent the case to the Venice Court of Appeals for a new judgment.

On October 20, 1989, four days before a new code of criminal procedure was to go into effect, the trial began before the Venice Court of Appeals. In 1990, for the first time in the history of Italian justice, the International Federation for Human Rights sent a number of experts as observers during the trial, including the chief of staff of the Paris police criminal laboratory, to ascertain the reliability of the forensic examinations.

Their report, which found in favor of the defendant, was not admitted into evidence due to procedural restrictions.

On December 22, 1990, after fourteen months of hearings, the court failed to hand down a judgment, issuing instead an interlocutory decree which sent the case to the Constitutional Court. The Venice court had found that one of the three new items of evidence was probative, and sustained, as its final judgment, that the defendant should be acquitted for insufficient evidence, but the court also stated that it could not enter final judgment in that it was unclear which code of criminal procedure should be applied.

On July 5, 1991, with an interpretive ruling published in the Official Gazette, the Constitutional Court decided that the Venice court ought to have applied the new code of criminal procedure and should have issued a full acquittal of Massimo Carlotto on December 22, 1990.

On February 21, 1992, after the Constitutional Court returned the court records, Carlotto's second appellate trial began before a new panel of judges because, in the meantime, the Chief Judge of the Venice Appeals Court had retired. The court decided to omit new evidentiary hearings, opting instead to adopt the previous evidentiary record through a summary reading of the earlier proceedings.

On March 27, 1992 the court confirmed the 1979 judgment of conviction and sentence, overturning the previous judgment on appeal.

On March 28, 1992, the Venice State Attorney's office issued an arrest warrant in compliance with that sentence.

On May 13, 1992, after forty-seven days in prison, Massimo Carlotto was again released due to serious health problems, and his sentence was deferred for one year.

On November 24, 1992, the Court of Cassation upheld the guilty verdict. That same evening, the possibility of a pardon was raised as the "only corrective instrument that could provide an equitable solution, closing this case in a humane and just manner." A further element in favor of a pardon was Massimo Carlotto's deteriorating state of health.

On November 25, 1992, less than twenty-four hours after the judgment, during a visit of the President of the Italian Republic to Padua, several members of the City Council presented him with a file on the case. During a public meeting with the citizenry, the President was asked about the possibility of a pardon, and he replied that he would examine the case with close attention.

On December 14, 1992, Massimo Carlotto's parents submitted a request for a pardon to the Court of Venice for a formal hearing preparatory to its official presentation to the President of the Republic.

The Solidarity Committees launched a campaign and a petition in support of the request for a pardon. They gathered eighteen thousand signatures in three months. The first person to sign the petition was the former Chief Justice of the Constitutional Court, Ettore Gallo. Throughout Italy, events, discussions, and performances were held; the Padua City Council approved a resolution in favor of the pardon.

On April 7, 1993, the President of the Republic, Oscar Luigi Scalfaro, granted a pardon to Massimo Carlotto.

ABOUT THE AUTHOR

Massimo Carlotto was born in Padua, Italy, and now lives in Sardinia. In addition to the many titles in his extremely popular Alligator series, he is also the author of *The Goodbye Kiss* and *Death's Dark Abyss* (Europa Editions, 2006). One of Italy's most popular authors and a major exponent of the Mediterranean noir novel, Carlotto has been compared with some of the most important American hardboiled crime writers. His novels have been translated into many languages, enjoying enormous success outside of Italy, and several have been made into highly acclaimed films.

About Europa Editions

"To insist that if work is good, no matter what, people will read it? Crazy! But perhaps that's why I like Europa . . . They believe in what they are doing above everything. Viva Europa Editions!"
—ALICE SEBOLD, author of *The Lovely Bones*

"A new and, on first evidence, excellent source for European fiction for English-speaking readers."—JANET MASLIN, *The New York Times*

"Europa Editions has its first indie bestseller, Elena Ferrante's *The Days of Abandonment*."—*Publishers Weekly*

"We certainly like what we've seen so far."—*The Complete Review*

"A distinctly different brand of literary pleasure, thoughtfulness and, yes, even entertainment."—*The Ruminator*

"You could consider Europa Editions, the sprightly new publishing venture [...] based in New York, as a kind of book club for Americans who thirst after exciting foreign fiction."—*LA Weekly*

"Europa Editions invites English-speaking readers to 'experience all the color, the exuberance, the violence, the sounds and smells of the Mediterranean,' with an intriguing selection of the crème de la crème of continental noir."—*Murder by the Bye*

"Readers with a taste—even a need—for an occasional inky cup of bitter honesty should lap up *The Goodbye Kiss* . . . the first book of Carlotto's to be published in the United States by the increasingly impressive new Europa Editions."—*Chicago Tribune*

www.europaeditions.com

www.europaeditions.com

The Days of Abandonment
Elena Ferrante
Fiction - 192 pp - $14.95 - isbn 1-933372-00-1

"Stunning . . . The raging, torrential voice of the author is something rare."—*The New York Times*

"I could not put this novel down. Elena Ferrante will blow you away."
—ALICE SEBOLD, author of *The Lovely Bones*

The gripping story of a woman's descent into devastating emptiness after being abandoned by her husband with two young children to care for.

Troubling Love
Elena Ferrante
Fiction - 144 pp - $14.95 - isbn 1-933372-16-8

"In tactile, beautifully restrained prose, Ferrante makes the domestic violence that tore [the protagonist's] household apart evident."—*Publishers Weekly*

"Ferrante has written the 'Great Neapolitan Novel.'"
—*Corriere della Sera*

Delia's voyage of discovery through the chaotic streets and claustrophobic sitting rooms of contemporary Naples in search of the truth about her mother's untimely death.

www.europaeditions.com

Cooking with Fernet Branca
James Hamilton-Paterson
Fiction - 288 pp - $14.95 - isbn 1-933372-01-X

"Provokes the sort of indecorous involuntary laughter that has more in common with sneezing than chuckling. Imagine a British John Waters crossed with David Sedaris."—*The New York Times*

Gerald Samper has his own private Tuscan hilltop where he wiles away his time working as a ghostwriter for celebrities and inventing wholly original culinary concoctions. His idyll is shattered by the arrival of Marta. A series of hilarious misunderstandings brings this odd couple into ever-closer proximity.

Old Filth
Jane Gardam
Fiction - 256 pp - $14.95 - isbn 1-933372-13-3

"This remarkable novel [...] will bring immense pleasure to readers who treasure fiction that is intelligent, witty, sophisticated and— a quality encountered all too rarely in contemporary culture— adult."—*The Washington Post*

The engrossing and moving account of the life of Sir Edward Feathers, from birth in colonial Malaya, to Wales, where he is sent as a "Raj orphan," to Oxford, his career and marriage, parallels much of the twentieth century's dramatic history.

www.europaeditions.com

Total Chaos
Jean-Claude Izzo
Fiction/Noir - 256 pp - $14.95 - isbn 1-933372-04-4

"Rich, ambitious and passionate . . . his sad, loving portrait of his native city is amazing."—*The Washington Post*

"Full of fascinating characters, tersely brought to life in a prose style that is (thanks to Howard Curtis's shrewd translation) traditionally dark and completely original."—*The Chicago Tribune*

The first installment in the Marseilles Trilogy.

Chourmo
Jean-Claude Izzo
Fiction/Noir - 256 pp - $14.95 - isbn 1-933372-17-6

"Like the best noir writers—and he is among the best—Izzo not only has a keen eye for detail but also digs deep into what makes men weep."—*Time Out New York*

Fabio Montale is dragged back into the mean streets of a violent, crime-infested Marseilles after the disappearance of his long lost cousin's teenage son.

www.europaeditions.com

The Goodbye Kiss
Massimo Carlotto
Fiction/Noir · 192 pp · $14.95 · isbn 1-933372-05-2

"A nasty, explosive little tome warmly recommended to fans of James M. Cain for its casual amorality and truly astonishing speed."—*Kirkus Reviews*

An unscrupulous womanizer, as devoid of morals now as he once was full of idealistic fervor, returns to Italy, where he is wanted for a series of crimes. To avoid prison he sells out his old friends, turns his back on his former ideals, and cuts deals with crooked cops. To earn himself the guise of respectability he is willing to go even further, maybe even as far as murder.

Death's Dark Abyss
Massimo Carlotto
Fiction/Noir · 192 pp · $14.95 · isbn 1-933372-18-4

"A narrative voice that in Lawrence Venuti's translation is cold and heartless—but, in a creepy way, fascinating."—*The New York Times*

A riveting drama of guilt, revenge, and justice, Massimo Carlotto's *Death's Dark Abyss* tells the story of two men and the savage crime that binds them. During a robbery, Raffaello Beggiato takes a young woman and her child hostage and later murders them. Beggiato is arrested, tried, and sentenced to life. The victims' father and husband, Silvano, plunges into a deepening abyss until the day the murderer seeks his pardon and he begins to plot his revenge.

www.europaeditions.com

Hangover Square
Patrick Hamilton
Fiction/Noir - 280 pp - $14.95 - isbn 1-933372-06-0

"Hamilton is a sort of urban Thomas Hardy: always a pleasure to read, and as social historian he is unparalleled."—NICK HORNBY

Adrift in the grimy pubs of London at the outbreak of World War II, George Harvey Bone is hopelessly infatuated with Netta, a cold, contemptuous small-time actress. George also suffers from occasional blackouts. During these moments one thing is horribly clear: he must murder Netta.

Boot Tracks
Matthew F. Jones
Fiction/Noir - 208 pp - $14.95 - isbn 1-933372-11-7

"More than just a very good crime thriller, this dark but illuminating novel shows us the psychopathology of the criminal mind . . . A nightmare thriller with the power to haunt."
—*Kirkus Reviews* (starred)

A commanding, stylishly written novel that tells the harrowing story of an assassination gone terribly wrong and the man and woman who are taking their last chance to find a safe place in a hostile world.

www.europaeditions.com

Love Burns
Edna Mazya
Fiction/Noir - 192 pp - $14.95 - isbn 1-933372-08-7

"This book, which has Woody Allen overtones, should be of great interest to readers of black humor and psychological thrillers."
—*Library Journal* (starred)

Ilan, a middle-aged professor of astrophysics, discovers that his young wife is having an affair. Terrified of losing her, he decides to confront her lover instead. Their meeting ends in the latter's murder—the unlikely murder weapon being Ilan's pipe—and in desperation, Ilan disposes of the body in the fresh grave of his kindergarten teacher. But when the body is discovered, the mayhem begins.

Departure Lounge
Chad Taylor
Fiction/Noir - 176 pp - $14.95 - isbn 1-933372-09-5

"Smart, original, surprising and just about as cool as a novel can get . . . Taylor can flat out write."—*The Washington Post*

A young woman mysteriously disappears. The lives of those she has left behind—family, acquaintances, and strangers intrigued by her disappearance—intersect to form a captivating latticework of coincidences and surprising twists of fate. Urban noir at its stylish and intelligent best.

www.europaeditions.com

The Big Question
Wolf Erlbruch
Children's Illustrated Fiction - 52 pp - $14.95 - isbn 1-933372-03-6

Named Best Book at the 2004 Children's Book Fair in Bologna.

"[*The Big Question*] offers more open-ended answers than the likes of Shel Silverstein's *Giving Tree* (1964) and is certain to leave even younger readers in a reflective mood."—*Kirkus Reviews*

A stunningly beautiful and poetic illustrated book for children that poses the biggest of all big questions: Why am I here?

The Butterfly Workshop
Wolf Erlbruch
Children's Illustrated Fiction - 40 pp - $14.95 - isbn 1-933372-12-5

Illustrated by the winner of the 2006 Hans Christian Andersen Award

For children and adults alike: Odair, one of the Designers of All Things and grandson of the esteemed inventor of the rainbow, has been banished to the insect laboratory as punishment for his over-active imagination. But he still dreams of one day creating a cross between a bird and a flower.

www.europaeditions.com

Carte Blanche
Carlo Lucarelli
Fiction/Noir - 120 pp - $14.95 - isbn 1-933372-15-X

"This is Alan Furst country, to be sure."—*Booklist*

The house of cards built by Mussolini in the last months of World War II is collapsing and Commissario De Luca faces a world mired in sadistic sex, dirty money, drugs and murder.

Dog Day
Alicia Giménez-Bartlett
Fiction/Noir - 208 pp - $14.95 - isbn 1-933372-14-1

"In Nicholas Caistor's smooth translation from the Spanish, Giménez-Bartlett evokes pity, horror and laughter with equal adeptness. No wonder she won the Femenino Lumen prize in 1997 as the best female writer in Spain."—*The Washington Post*

Delicado and her maladroit sidekick, Garzón, investigate the murder of a tramp whose only friend is a mongrel dog named Freaky.